THE WARRIORS OF WHISKEY CITY

Book Six
in
The Whiskey City
Series

THE WARRIORS
OF
WHISKEY CITY

Book Six
in
The Whiskey City
Series

•

ROBIN GIBSON

AVALON BOOKS
THOMAS BOUREGY AND COMPANY, INC.
401 LAFAYETTE STREET
NEW YORK, NEW YORK 10003

W
GIBSON
c. 1

PRINTED IN THE UNITED STATES OF AMERICA
ON ACID-FREE PAPER
BY HADDON CRAFTSMEN, SCRANTON, PENNSYLVANIA

THE WARRIORS OF WHISKEY CITY

Book Six
in
The Whiskey City
Series

/

Chapter One

The town of Whiskey City, Wyoming, lay sleeping under a blanket of stars. Not a sound, nor even a breath of wind, stirred in the peaceful town. Just over a mile away, not yet in sight of the town, a man rode slowly, slumped over the saddle. The man's face was haggard and tired as he clung to the back of his horse and to his life with the tenacity of a drowning man.

The horse wasn't his, he'd stolen it. It wasn't the fact that he had stolen a horse—or the twin bullets lodged in his body—that made the man swivel painfully in the saddle and glance behind him. This man didn't fear what his pursuers would do if they caught him. They would kill him; he accepted that. Boris Fedarov was ready to die.

All that mattered was that he reach his comrades and warn them. Groaning from the pain the movement caused, Fedarov patted his pocket, making sure the letters were still there. He must deliver them to Dmitri and Vanya. Fedarov could only hope his friends had already reached Whiskey City.

As the dark, hulking shapes of the buildings that made up the town came slowly into view, Fedarov coughed, a smile coming to his bloodstained lips. He'd made it. Now, Czar Alexander of Russia would die, as he deserved.

The sound his horse's hooves made as they struck the hard-packed street sounded loud to Boris Fedarov. They pounded at his aching head. Groaning, he guided his stolen horse down the center of the street until he saw a sign proclaiming that building to be the hotel. Urging the horse over to the boardwalk, Fedarov slid from the saddle.

Holding an arm across his stomach, Fedarov drew his pistol. Hitching along, he entered the hotel, stopping in the center of the darkened lobby. Fedarov scowled. How would he know which room his friends were in?

Boris Fedarov had no wish to wake everyone in the place by knocking on every door, but he intended to find Dmitri and Vanya. Boris Fedarov was determined that his mission not fail, not after what he'd already been through.

A door opened off to his left, and a woman holding a candle stepped into the lobby. Fedarov saw the movement and tried to turn and raise his gun, but his weary legs gave out and he crashed to the floor. A stab of pain shot through him; he had failed. That sheriff and Arkady Rostov were going to catch him. Boris Fedarov didn't know Sheriff Cooper, but he knew Arkady Rostov. Rostov's appointment as head of the Royal Guards had been no fluke. The man took his duties seriously, he would gladly die to protect one of the Romanov family. Boris Fedarov knew that for what he had done, Rostov would chase him to the ends of the earth.

He had to get up! Rostov would be coming. Gritting his teeth, Fedarov tried to push his battered body off the floor. He managed to lever himself to his knees, but his weakened muscles would take no more punishment. With a groan, he slumped back to the floor. Fedarov's last thought was that he had failed miserably. That sheriff and

Rostov were going to catch him. They were already closing in.

That weren't nowhere near true. I'm the sheriff of Whiskey City, and at that time, me and my friends weren't in shape to be chasing a gimpy turtle. The battle we'd had with Fedarov and his goons left us sucking for air. We'd whupped Fedarov and his boys, but they sure enough got in some licks of their own. We had two wounded men on our hands, Arkady Rostov and Ferrell Cauruthers. Both had been wounded and were in no shape to travel. Besides, we were a couple of horses short.

Carrying an armload of wood, I limped up to the fire. Naw, I hadn't been shot, but I'd walked about a thousand miles with a hole blasted through the sole of my boot. Now, I'm a big man, and walking don't come easy to me any time, but with a hole in my boot? Well, that made stomping across the county pure torture. I swear, the bottom of my paw was raw as a Dodge City steak.

My friends, Bobby Stamper and Louey Claude hunkered around our fire, their hands wrapped around a pair of coffee cups. I dropped the wood beside the fire and sank to the ground beside it. Right then, I felt like I could sleep a week.

Mr. Claude looked up and I noticed the little farmer's face was drawn and tired. It hit me all at once, Louey was no longer a young man. "Come morning, we should move everyone over to Karl's," Claude suggested.

Now, he had a point. I'd been thinking in terms of packing the whole crew into town, but Karl Wiesmulluer's place was a sight closer. Besides, if we went to Wiesmulluer's, I could see his daughter, Eddy. Me and Eddy were fixing to get married, just as soon as we got around to it.

"Me and Louey could head out now," Bobby suggested, bounding to his feet. "We could pick up a wagon and be back by noon," he predicted with a confident grin.

I glanced irritably at Bobby. He was my best friend, but sometimes he got on my nerves. I mean, my tail was dragging lower than a gopher's basement, and here he was all full of pep and grinning like he was having a ball. Didn't hardly seem fair to me. Still, he had a point. With a groan I pushed myself to my feet. "All right, I'll help you saddle up," I agreed tiredly. The sooner we got those wounded men off our hands, the better I would feel.

I helped Bobby and Louey saddle a couple of horses. As they rode away, I went to check on the wounded men. I was hoping to find Ferrell Cauruthers awake. I had a few questions to ask that hombre.

I could read trail sign as well as most. And judging from the tracks we'd found around the wrecked stage, I was sure Cauruthers was one of them that had held up the stage, kidnapped that duchess, and shot the driver. The thing that had befuddled me was that when we finally caught up to them, Cauruthers was helping that duchess. Fact is, if he hadn't pitched in when he did, Fedarov's gang might have turned the tables on us.

As I knelt beside the two wounded men, I found that both Cauruthers and Arkady Rostov seemed to be resting easy, so I didn't figure they would croak on us.

Straightening up, I glanced at the small fire where the princess was bedded down. I figured I could ask that princess, but to tell the truth, I'd seen the moon-eyed looks she'd been giving Cauruthers and wasn't right sure she'd tell the truth. 'Course, I was the law in these parts, and I figured I had a right to know what the devil was going on.

Right then, I decided to ask her a few questions, and she'd better tell me the truth. I was walking over to where she had her blankets spread out when I ran belly-first into the business end of a rifle.

"Halt! Who goes there?" Lester bellered, prodding me with that danged rifle.

I weren't in any mood for any catywhumpussing around. My patience was worn as thin as bunkhouse porridge. Not that you can blame me. I mean, in the last few days, I'd been shot at, chased that princess halfway across the country, and just to top things off, my foot felt like I had a porcupine in my boot. Besides, I'd had dealings with Lester and his brother Elmo before, and on their best day, they weren't nothing but a royal pain in the hind end.

So when Lester gouged me with that rifle, my temper shot right through the rafters. With a roar, I slapped that rifle away, and was ready to bat him in the whiskers for good measure, when another rifle gouged me in the back.

"He said halt, clubfoot!" Elmo shrieked, stepping out of the shadows.

"What the devil has got into you two meatheads!" I sputtered. Like I said, I had dealings with these two before, and was well aware of the fact that they weren't near the sharpest two galoots, but this was stretching it, even for them. I was fixin' to bark some hide off their noggins when Princess Catrinia interrupted.

"Elmo, what seems to be the problem?" she asked, gliding up beside Elmo. Now, for a young woman who'd been jerked off a stage and drug halfway across the country, this princess or duchess or whatever she was stood it mighty well. She didn't look nothing like the bedraggled waif we'd rescued this afternoon. She'd done some rakin' at her hair and some scrubbing on her face. Right then, with a little pink glow on her cheeks, she looked like a princess. A feathery smile gracing her delicate face, she placed a slim hand on Elmo's shoulder. "What is the problem?"

His long face red, Elmo glared at me and spat on the ground. "We caught this overgrown varmint trying to sneak up on you," Elmo allowed, then gouged me with that rifle. "Ya want me to plug him?"

I reckon even the wax in my ears was boiling, 'cause I was ready to explode. My hands balled into fists, I was pawing the ground when I heard that princess laugh.

"I doubt if that will be necessary," she said, a twinkle in her eye.

"You sure," Elmo growled, poking at me

with the rifle. "I wouldn't trust the overgrown varmint no farther than I could throw him."

"It's okay, I imagine the sheriff has some questions he wishes to ask me," she said, patting Elmo's arm. "Why don't you and Lester retire for the evening. I'm sure I'll be safe with the sheriff."

"Well, all right," Elmo grumbled as Lester picked up his rifle. "But don't you get any notions, bigfoot. Me and Lester are right light sleepers. You try anything and I'll ventilate you real quick!"

"Try anything?" I howled. What the devil was I gonna try? I mean, I'd just run my tail off, trying to save the old gal. My temper bubbling like frying grease, I took a step at them two brothers, sputtering as I tried to come up with the words that fit the occasion. Oh, I had a few in mind, but they weren't nothing I could say in front of a lady. Finally, I settled for growling and shaking my fist at them.

"We're gonna be keeping an eye on you," Elmo warned as his brother nodded several times. Shooting me hard looks, they backed away.

As the two brothers slunk back into the shadows, I turned to the princess, rubbing a spot between my eyes, which was starting to ache something fierce. Dealing with those two could drive a preacher to drink. "What in the world has got into them?" I demanded.

Princess Catrinia laughed, motioning for me to have a seat beside the fire. "They were just taking their jobs seriously."

"Jobs? What do you mean, jobs?"

"I hired them," she said simply. "They are going to be my new bodyguards."

I was plumb flabbergasted. I couldn't even cuss, and believe me, I wanted to. "You hired them two?" I stammered. I cocked my head, looking at her close to see if she was goofed in the head. "Ma'am, have you been snorting turpentine?"

"No," she said, with a delicate laugh. "I can assure you that I am in full possession of my faculties."

Now, I ain't right certain what that meant, but if it meant she was loco, I believed it. Anyone that would hire Lester and Elmo just didn't have all their hogs in one pen. Why, I'd just as soon squat on a nest of rattlers as trust them two.

"Did you wish to ask me some questions?"

"Huh? Oh, yeah," I muttered, shaking my head to get my notions back on the right trail. "I wanted to ask you about that Cauruthers hombre. The way I read the tracks, he was one of them that shanghaied you off that stagecoach."

"Yes, he was," Princess Catrinia said, her eyes drifting off, looking through the darkness to where Ferrell Cauruthers lay sleeping. All of a sudden, her face got all swoopy, and her eyes glassed over like a man who'd been mule kicked. "He was tricked into helping Boris Fedarov. As soon as Ferrell realized his mistake, he tried to help me."

"This Fedarov, is he the jasper that got away?"

"Yes," Catrinia replied softly, a look of fear springing to her eyes. "Boris means to assassinate my father. You must help me stop him."

Now I figured that was Rostov's job, seeing as how he was the head of the Royal Palace Guards, or whatever that highfalutin title was he was always jabbering about. 'Course, Rostov wasn't in shape to rassle a titmouse, so I reckoned the job of snagging this Fedarov was gonna fall to me.

Well, I'd already promised that I would help her, but I was starting to wish I'd looked before I leaped. I had no earthly idea what I'd gotten myself into, but from what I'd seen of them Russians, I didn't reckon I was gonna like it. I mean, up till now, I'd never even met a Russian, and now, all of a sudden, they were crawling over the country like ants. In the last few days, I'd met up with six or seven Russkies, and most of them done their level best to kill me. The ones that didn't shoot at me tried bossing me around like they thought I was their camp boy or something. Yes, sir, I was fed to the teeth with Russians.

And if Lester and Elmo were mixed up in the deal, I figured it'd be easier just to shoot myself now and save a lot of riding. Now, as those thoughts sorta trickled through my skull, I had no idea how close to the truth they would turn out to be. What I didn't know was that my troubles was just starting. In a few days, I'd be viewing these as good times.

Boris Fedarov woke slowly, a fuzzy feeling in his head and on his tongue. Raising his head, he glanced about the room, trying to remember just where he was.

He lay in a small, hard bed in a plain little room. Fedarov had no recollection of the room, nor the sad-looking woman who was folding his suits into a dresser drawer. "Where am I?" he croaked.

The woman jumped, spinning around swiftly. "Oh, you're awake," she said, backing toward the door.

Fedarov licked his dry, cracked lips. "I'm awake, but I do not know where I am."

"Oh, yes, of course," the woman said, patting a loose strand of brown hair back into her bun as she continued to edge toward the door. "You're in the hotel. My husband and I own this place. My name is Imogene Fowler. I found you in the lobby last night. You'd been shot. You were riding Bobby Stamper's horse," she said, the last part coming out like an accusation.

Boris Fedarov ignored the tone in her voice, grimacing in pain as he sat up. "Then I made it to Whiskey City?"

"Yes," Imogene Fowler said sternly. "How did you happen to come by Bobby's horse?"

This time, Fedarov was alerted by the hard edge of suspicion in her voice. He took his time answering, trying to think of a story she might believe. "I was looking for the Grand Duchess Catrinia Romanov when my men and I were attacked. My men were wiped out, but I managed to catch that horse and escape with my life."

"Who were the men that attacked you?"

Fedarov could sense her suspicion slipping and shook his head sadly. "I do not know, but they were a rough, unscrupulous lot of blackguards. I pray that they are not the ones who abducted Catrinia, but I fear they were."

Imogene Fowler frowned, chewing on a fingernail. "I wonder how those men came to have Bobby's horse?" A horrified look sprang to her face as she covered her mouth with her hand. "You don't suppose they attacked Bobby and stole his horse?"

Fedarov wanted to smile, but he only nodded grimly. "I'm afraid so. As I said, these were despicable men. They attacked us in a most cowardly fashion," Fedarov lied, knowing from Imogene's expression that she was buying his story. "I am sorry. I can see this Bobby was a friend of yours. I regret your loss."

Mrs. Fowler nodded and blew her nose. "You must be hungry. Would you like something to eat?"

"You are very kind," Fedarov replied. "Also, I am seeking to find two of my countrymen, Dmitri Grazovitch and Vanya Drago. Do you know if they are in town?"

"There are a couple of Russian gentlemen in town. I don't recall their names, but I can inquire if you wish."

"You are indeed an angel," Fedarov replied, leaning back into his pillows. "I just hope that someday, I am in a position to re-pay you for your graciousness."

"Thank nothing of it, Mr . . . ," Imogene started.

"Fedarov, Boris Fedarov. I am the adviser to the czar."

"You must be an important man in Russia."

"Important enough to be trusted with the welfare of the czar's daughter." Fedarov struggled to set up. "I must find my friends so we can rescue the princess!"

"You rest," Mrs. Fowler said hurriedly. "I'll go check on your friends. If they are in Whiskey City, I shall find them."

As Imogene Fowler left, Fedarov relaxed, smoothing the blanket with his hands. Per-haps all was not lost. He had the letters he'd forced Catrinia to write, urging her father to come to San Francisco for the official cere-mony that would officially transfer owner-ship of Alaska to the United States.

Catrinia's father, Alexander, could be lured to San Francisco, and Fedarov had the men lined up to kill the czar, but he had no money to pay his killers. When he had Ca-trinia kidnapped, Fedarov planned to use her ransom to pay his assassins. Of course, he had no intention of letting Catrinia live.

For years, Boris Fedarov had served the Romanov family, but he hated them. He'd watched them parading around in their silk gowns and fancy suits while his own family struggled to survive. Boris Fedarov's father had worked his whole life in the royal stables, spending his time cleaning up after the horses of the Romanovs. Boris himself had grown up wearing clothes cast off by the royal family. Even now, as he recalled the shame of it, a red flush crept up his neck and spread across his face. They would pay!

For years, Boris had planned this. He had worked hard serving the czar, moving up until he was a trusted servant and adviser, all the time waiting for his chance.

He wanted to kill them all, but he would settle for Alexander and Catrinia. For a brief, wonderful second, Catrinia had been in his grasp, but she had escaped. Next time, he vowed, she would not be so lucky.

As Fedarov thought about it a rage came over him. He ground his teeth and glared at the cracked ceiling over his head. If it had not been for that sheriff and his friends, Fedarov's plan would have worked. Fedarov clenched his fists, a vein in his neck standing out. He owed the men who had helped the duchess a debt of blood, and he intended to pay it off in full.

Chapter Two

Three days passed quickly as Boris Fedarov rested and healed. True to her word, Imogene Fowler had been most helpful. She had found his friends, Dmitri Grazovitch and Vanya Drago. They now sat in chairs beside Fedarov's bed.

The pair were as different as the seasons, but they worked well together. Huge and hulking Vanya Drago provided the muscle and the passion, while the smaller Dmitri was the cool brains of the partnership.

Fedarov listened to his companions and knew they were ready to leave Whiskey City. It was time to go, before the authorities showed up.

Fedarov knew this, but he did not know if

he could travel. Three days of rest had greatly improved his condition, but he was still sore and weak. Fedarov didn't know if he could stand the trip, but he knew it was either try or be left behind. In Russia, Fedarov would be quickly shot if he were captured, and he expected no less here.

"It is time," Drago said, his tone harsh. "Soon that sheriff you spoke of will return and we must be gone. If you cannot travel, you must be left behind."

Fedarov nodded; he understood. "When?" he asked.

Drago and Grazovitch exchanged a look. "It must be in the morning," Dmitri Grazovitch said. "The letters have been sent; everything is ready."

"What about the money? We must have much money to pay the men who would kill the czar," Fedarov said.

Dmtri smiled. "There are those in the American government who wish us to succeed. When I rode to the place called Central City to mail the letters, I contacted these people by telegraph. They have assured us that the money will be made available once we reach San Francisco. This town shall provide us with the rest of what we need."

"You rest now, my friend," Grazovitch said

quietly. "We have a long, arduous journey ahead of us. You must have your strength. We cannot afford to be slowed down."

Fedarov nodded to his two companions. He knew what they meant. "Have no fear. I shall be ready," he promised.

Very early the next morning, as a ceiling of dark clouds hung over Whiskey City, the three Russians crept soundlessly from the hotel. As they stole down the street under the cover of darkness, the Russians did not resemble men setting about honest business. Looking like thieves in the night, they slunk down the street, lurking in the shadows next to the buildings.

Boris Fedarov hobbled slowly behind his two companions, his teeth clenched against the pain. Concentrating on fighting the stabbing pain that shot through his body with each step, Boris paid little attention to what was going on around him. He gripped the rifle he carried and made himself a vow: Czar Alexander would know such pain as this before he died.

As his friends stopped in front of Gid Stevens's store, Fedarov's breathing was hoarse and his face gray. A word passed between Drago and Grazovitch that Boris did not catch, nor care about.

Drago grunted, then raised his rifle, using the butt to slash the lock off the door. "Boris, you keep watch while Dmitri and I gather the things we shall need," Vanya Drago said, making the request sound like an order.

Glad for the rest, Fedarov sank into the low bench outside the store. His rifle lying lightly across his knees, Fedarov watched the street while his friends plundered the store. Growing up hungry in Russia made them efficient looters. In less than five minutes, they hurried from the store, their arms loaded with supplies. "Let's go," Grazovitch whispered, hurriedly leading the way to the stable.

While Drago and Grazovitch saddled the horses, Fedarov worked stiffly, packing the supplies into saddlebags. Drago cinched the last saddle into place, then passed the reins to Fedarov. "We have one last duty to perform," he whispered. "Take the horses out into the street and wait for us."

Without a backward glance, he and Grazovitch walked from the stable, their destination a small frame house behind the bank. Like an army rolling across the countryside, they stalked up to the house. Without a word, Drago broke down the door and rushed inside.

The crash of the front door woke Milton Andrews from a deep sleep. His eyes still bleary, he saw the large, silent figures rushing through the darkness at him. Bleating with fear, Milt fumbled in the nightstand for the ancient pistol he kept there.

Drago sprang upon poor Milt before his stubby fingers could find the weapon. Slashing out with a rough fist, Drago knocked the banker to the floor. "Please, do not hurt me," Milt whimpered as he tried desperately to crawl under the bed. Milt could smell the kerosine from a broken lamp and feel the sharp slivers of glass slicing his skin, but he frantically kept crawling.

Drago snatched Andrews by the back of his nightshirt and picked him bodily from the floor, slamming him against the wall. His teeth bared, Drago pressed his pistol cruelly against the banker's cheek. "Do as we say or I shall kill you," he whispered. "Do you understand?"

"Yes," Andrews whimpered. A tremor passed through his body as he stared into the cold gray eyes of his attacker. "Please, do not kill me."

"Whether we leave you dead or alive is entirely up to you," Grazovitch said, crowding up close to the pair. "Now, you shall come with us."

"Where are we going?"

Drago's teeth flashed again as he smiled, grinding the pistol even deeper into Andrews's cheek. "Why, to your bank, of course," he said, pulling the banker away from the wall and pointing him in the direction of the door. "Now, move!"

Sniveling, Andrews tried to pick his way delicately across the glass strewn on the floor, but Drago kept pushing him. By the time they reached the door, Milt's feet were bleeding badly from a dozen cuts.

No mercy in his heart, Drago ruthlessly herded Milt across the alley to the bank, slamming his rifle into Milt's back every time the banker faltered. "Open it," he ordered when they reached the back door.

"I can't," Milt stammered, then cringed away as Drago raised his arm to strike. "Please, I don't have the keys. They're at home."

Drago shook Andrews and swore viciously. He glanced at Grazovitch, knowing they had made a mistake. Grazovitch met his partners stare, then shrugged. Raising a heavy boot, he kicked the door open.

"Inside!" Drago hissed, bodily shoving Milt

inside. "Open the safe! Do it now!" he said, raising his pistol to back up the order.

His wide eyes glued to the pistol, Milt stumbled into his office, kneeling before the safe. A tremor shaking his lips, Milt reached for the dial. His hands shook so badly that Milt messed up the combination twice.

"Idiot!" Drago screamed, slapping the pudgy banker. First with his palm, then the back of his hand, Drago rained heavy blows onto the face of Milton Andrews. "Open it or die!" Drago said, his chest heaving from the exertion.

Tears mixing with the blood running from the cuts Drago's ring had opened up, Milton tried again. This time, the lock responded to his touch, and when he turned the lever, the door swung silently open.

Grunting an exclamation, Drago dragged Andrews back from the safe. Opening a heavy canvas bag, Grazovitch took Milt's place in front of the safe. Working feverishly, Grazovitch raked money into the bag.

Halfway done, Dmitri Grazovitch paused, glancing over his shoulder. "Dispose of that," he said, jerking his head to indicate Andrews.

"Da!" Drago said, a smile touching his lips as he ran his hands lightly over his pistol.

*   *   *

From a distance, the town looked peaceful, sunning itself on a beautiful day under a cloudless afternoon. I shoulda known right then that something was wrong; Whiskey City ain't never peaceful.

Bobby and I rode slowly into town. Mr. Burdett, who ran the livery stable, and Joe Havens, who ran the saloon, met us in the middle of the street. I frowned as I saw them, They were packing enough shooting irons to start a war.

"Teddy, where the devil have you been?" Joe snarled.

I shot a puzzled look at Bobby, who shrugged and started rolling himself a smoke. "I was out at Wiesmulluer's place, helping that princess," I explained. "What went wrong?"

"The bank was robbed!" Burdett exclaimed.

"Robbed?" Bobby and I said together. "How? What happened?" I sputtered.

Joe scowled at me and scratched the dirty stripe of grime spread across the belly of his shirt. Years of leaning against his bar while he griped and poured drinks had ground that stain in permanently. Not that the rest of his wardrobe was all that clean. In fact, the sleeve of his shirt got a mite filthier as he dragged it over his mouth in a quick, angry swipe, smearing tobacco juice down the sleeve. "They jerked ol' Andrews outta bed and made him open the safe," Joe said, then spat in the street. "They had to torture him a good bit to get him to do it too. His feet were cut up something terrible."

"Is he gonna be all right?" Bobby asked.

Joe shrugged. "They gave him a right smart pistol-whipping. He ain't woke up yet. Don't know if he ever will."

"A skull fracture is a most serious wound," Burdett agreed gravely. "A lot of folks never pull through something like that."

I was worried now. I mean, at one time or another, Burdett had had most every ailment and affliction that a man can catch. I figured he knew what he was talking about.

"You going after them?" Joe demanded, interrupting my thoughts.

"Yeah," I said, rubbing my chin. "Any idea who done this?"

Joe swore. "Shoot, yes, I know! It was them Russians!"

I raised an eyebrow and shot a glance at Bobby. "Russians?"

"Yeah," Joe growled. "There was three of them nested up over at the hotel. Now, I tried to tell Fowler they was no good, and that he oughta boot them out, but Imogene wouldn't hear of it. Said they was nice men," he added with a hooting laugh.

"You are going after them?" Burdett asked worried. "We can't afford to lose all that money."

"Yeah, I'll go after them," I said, then looked to Bobby for help.

"We could use some help," Bobby said.

"I can't go," Burdett said immediately. "I been feeling poorly. I reckon I'm coming down with whooping cough or something," he complained, then hacked out a couple of measly little coughs.

"How about you, Joe?" I pressed.

Joe grimaced, like I'd walloped him one. "Can't you get somebody else?"

"Who?" Bobby demanded.

"There's Gid Stevens," Burdett suggested.

Joe laughed harshly and spat into the dirt. "You know Gid won't be allowed to go. Since he got hitched, he can't get outta the shadow of Iris's skirttails."

"That just leaves you, Joe," I pointed out. "How about it?"

"I ain't hardly got the time," he complained. "Besides, who'd watch the saloon?"

"Close it up," Bobby suggested. "Think of how thirsty folks will be when you get back."

Joe thrust back his shoulders and set his feet in the dirt like a balky mule. I almost smiled. I'd known Joe Havens my whole life, and I knew him well enough to know he was going with us. Joe might beller and holler like a squashed hog, but when a body needed a hand, Joe was always there. "Please, Joe, as a favor to me," I said, then patted him on the shoulder. "I could use your help."

"Dadgum, kids," he mumbled, looking down at the street as he pawed his boots into the dust. "Aw, all right," he said with a groan, giving in and not looking too happy about it. "I reckon somebody has to tag along so you two don't get lost."

"Good," I said, swinging down and handing my reins to Burdett. "Saddle us up some fresh horses. We'll stock up some supplies and leave in an hour."

It took a mite more than an hour. Joe insisted on packing half of the store with us. At first I thought we had way too many supplies, but after a few days, I began to wonder if we had enough. I swear, Joe ate like a boar hog with a tapeworm. Still, we made good time and closed the gap some.

Ten days out of Whiskey City, we pulled

up and studied the tracks. We'd rode like the
devil hisself was on our heels and we'd closed
the gap a bunch. We stopped just shy of sun-
down on that tenth day, and I figured we
weren't more than two hours behind them.
As usual, Joe was griping and wanted to stop,
but I had other ideas. The way I saw it, if we
pushed on, we might catch them sleeping.
Besides, I had my own coons to tree, and
wanted this whole business to be over with.

"Be awful easy to lose the trail in the dark,"
Joe warned when I explained my notion.

"If we got off track, we could pick it up
again in the morning. They're leaving a trail
a blind dog could foller," I argued. "I figure if
we keep going a couple more hours, we ought
to find their camp. Maybe we could sneak up
on them while they're sleeping."

Joe never liked it, but me and Bobby over-
ruled him, and we pushed on. We needn't
have worried about losing the trail; after an
hour, we caught the glow of their campfire.
Not that it was any great feat, they had a fire
big enough to see four counties away. I'll say
one thing, if they kept building fires like that,
we wouldn't have to worry about them Russians. A man hunkered over a fire of that
size was liable to get an arrow through his
gizzard.

We pulled up about a little less than a mile from their camp, in a low, bare washout. "Let's wait, give them awhile to go to sleep, then jump them," I suggested.

"Sounds good," Bobby said, sliding off his horse. He stretched out his back against a tree and tipped his hat over his eyes. "Call me when you're ready."

"Yeah, me too," Joe grumbled, finding himself a place to nap.

While they slept, I led the horses away, staking them out to graze. I started to unsaddle the horses, but then changed my mind. I sure enough figured we could take them Russians, but a body never knew. If the fight went against us, we might have to make a run for it. Best leave the saddles on our horses just in case.

Tying the horses loosely, so they could graze, I snuck up closer, where I could see the Russians' camp. Now, I'll say one thing for them Russkies, they might be roughing it, but they were doing it in grand style. Why, they were eating their grub off real plates, using eating irons and dabbing at their mouths with what looked like hunks of flour sack.

After they finished their chow, they proceeded to wash dang near everything in camp. I'll be darned if they didn't up and shuck their duds and wash them too. I had to shake my head. I never saw the like. Most times a body has trouble keeping his bloomers dry. He sure don't wet them up a'purpose.

They slipped on some shiny looking drawers and then turned in for the night. By the time they settled in, my own eyes were drooping like the jowls of a coon hound, but I figured to give them a few more minutes to saunter off into dream land. I waited until their fire was dying out, and I was sure they were snoozing. Then I scooted back to our camp. I ghosted back to our makeshift camp, making no more noise than a titmouse crossing a frozen pond. I reached out a hand to shake Bobby awake, but my hand closed over the cold steel of a pistol barrel. "They asleep?" Bobby asked, flipping that six-gun back into the holster. Even in the dark, I could see his teeth flashing.

"Yeah," I said with a grunt, sore as a mashed thumb. It peeved me to no end that he had heard me coming. Now, I reckon Bobby Stamper is about the best friend I ever had, but sometimes I got tired of always looking like hand-me-downs around him. "Go wake up Joe," I said, growling as I checked my pistol.

Bobby's way of waking Joe was simply kicking him in the keister with the toe of his boot. I don't know if was the boot in the britches, or just that he was naturally grouchy, but Joe came out of his nap prickly as a barrel cactus.

"Would you quit your bellyaching," I hissed at him. "You want to wake them up?"

"Aw, shut your yap. I was hunting down thieves when you was still hiding behind your mama's skirttails," Joe grumbled, pulling a bottle from his pocket. He took a healthy snort, then belched and scratched his belly. "How's about something to eat? I'm hungry."

"Hungry?" I said, shaking my head. "We can eat after we catch them."

"They ain't going anywhere," Joe grumbled. "I say we have something to eat first. I never do my best fighting on an empty belly."

"I could use something to eat myself," Bobby said, taking sides with Joe. "Like he said, they're stopped for the night. Ain't no use in getting in a rush."

I just shook my head. I mean, I'm a man who likes his vittles. Most times I'm ready to belly up to the table and do my fair share, but I didn't reckon now was the time. We'd chased these jaspers ten whole days, and now that we had them Russkies right in our sights, Bobby and Joe wanted to stop and eat. I didn't want to give in, but my own belly was reminding me that we hadn't eaten all day. Besides, I knew how stubborn them two could be. "All right, but don't take all night."

As Bobby set about building a fire, Joe pulled out his bottle again. He took a long, gurgling drink, then started to stuff the bottle back into his pocket. Right then a snort sounded mighty friendly, so I stepped up and jerked the bottle from his hand.

His cry of protest was drowned out by the sound of a gunshot. I felt a blinding wave of pain in my face, then heard several more shots as I tumbled to the ground.

Chapter Three

As I fell, a bullet snatched the hat from my head, whipping it off into the night. I hit the ground in a heap, my face and eyes burning like lye soap. The whole side of my face stung something fierce, and I could feel something wet running down my face, and knew I'd been shot in the head. It wasn't until some of that liquid rolled down into my mouth that I realized it wasn't blood, but cheap whiskey.

Soon as I figured out I wasn't about to die, I got good and mad. I hauled out my pistol and commenced to blazing away. I could hear Joe and Bobby shooting as well. For a minute there, it was like being high in the mountains during a lightning storm. There were flashes and booms all around me, and the bullets were flying through the air like locusts. I don't know who ambushed us, but they sure enough had us dead to rights. Not that I figured on going down easy. I was in a bad mood, and a little scrap suited me just fine. Still, I knew that unless we pulled something mighty fancy out of the bag, they was gonna salt us.

Down in that little holler like we was, all they had to do was keep us pinned down till morning. Once the sun came up, they could pick us off one by one. The shooting tapered off as everyone had to reload. I rolled sideways several feet, then commenced to plugging fresh shells into my shooter.

I just got it poured full and was searching the darkness for a target, when a bawling cry cut through the night. "Whoeee! I got one! That big galoot went down like he'd been pole-axed!"

As that cry died away, my first instinct was to bang my head into the ground. Then my temper went off like a keg of blasting powder. "Lester!" I howled, slobbering spit in front of me. "What the devil do you think you are doing?"

For a long second, the night got quiet as death. "Sheriff Teddy," Lester called out uncertainly. "Is that you?"

I done some cussin', yes, sir, I surely did. I swear, when they was handing out brains, these two musta got the runts of the litter, if they got any at all. "Dang right it's me!" I screamed, shouting myself hoarse. "Who'd you think it would be?" I yelled, surging to my feet.

Lester stood up, and even through the gloom, I could see him scratching his head. "We thought you was them there Russkies."

"Careful, Lester. It's liable to be a trick," Elmo said, then shouted down to us. "How do we know it's really you?" he asked as Bobby laughed.

"I'm gonna trick you upside the head," I said, fuming and glaring the laugh right off Bobby's face. "Now, get down here!" I yelled, taking a step at them.

I barely took that step before I heard the shot and felt the bullet whip past me. "You just hold it right there," Elmo called. "I ain't made up my mind about you yet."

"I swear, I'm gonna throttle the both of them," I vowed, still hugging the ground. "Don't shoot, I'm just going over to the fire," I yelled, climbing cautiously to my feet. Half expecting one of them nitwits to shoot me, I crossed to the fire. I bent down and picked up a burning stick, holding it close to my face. "Now, can you see it's me?"

"Yeah," I reckon it's you, all right," Elmo said, sounding disappointed that he wasn't gonna get to shoot anyone. He stood up slowly, pointing his rifle down at us. "Okay, the rest of you can get up now, but don't make any sudden moves."

"Joe, go check the horses, I'm going to see about our friends," Bobby said, springing to his feet.

As Elmo and Lester stumbled sheepishly into our camp, I paced, chomping my teeth together. Right then, I was plumb flabbergasted. I couldn't even speak, I was so mad. All I could do was contemplate how good it would feel to bend my rifle barrel over their pointy little heads.

Joe came rushing in from checking the horses, and he sure wasn't at a loss for words. "They're gone!" he shouted, flapping his arms in the air.

A cold feeling of dread batted me right in the whiskers. This here wasn't the country you wanted to be afoot in. "The horses are gone?" I asked, hoping he'd been talking about something else.

"Gone, along with all our stuff!" Joe screamed. He wiped his foaming mouth with a quick swipe of his hand, then turned a scalding gaze on the two brothers. "I say we kill them here and now, and dump their bodies in a river."

Now, for a gawky, scrawny cuss, Elmo had a bonnet full of bluster packed into him. He bucked right up against Joe. "Yeah, tubby, and who's gonna help you?"

I reckon Joe was riled enough to throttle Elmo with his bare hands, but I snatched Elmo by the collar and dragged him back. "Shut up," I said, shaking Elmo a mite. "Where's your horses?"

"Good idea, Teddy," Joe said. "After we kill them, we'll be needing their horses."

Now, I wasn't about to kill them, nor let Joe do it, although I did savor the thought for a second or two. 'Course, I didn't have nothing agin scaring them a bit. I placed my hands on my hips and gave them a dose of my best no-nonsense look. "Where's your horses?" I demanded.

Elmo crossed his arms over his chest and stuck his lower lip out about a foot. "We ain't saying."

A man can take only so much, and I'd had aplenty. I snatched Elmo back up by the scruff of the neck and shook him but good. "I ain't asking again. Where's your horses?"

"I ain't gonna say!" Elmo brayed, then promptly mashed my toes with the heel of his boot.

"Yeeow!" Bellering like a constipated moose, I danced around on one foot. I swear, if that danged Elmo woulda been closer, I woulda bashed his head in. "Dang your sorry hide, Elmo. We need your horses to round up ours," I screeched at him.

"Too late for that," Bobby said quietly from the edge of our camp. "Them horses spooked right into the Russians' camp. They got 'em now."

"All of them?" I asked, gingerly setting some weight back on my injured foot.

Bobby shrugged, leaning against a tree and rolling himself a smoke. "I couldn't see for sure, but they got both packhorses and at least two of the saddle horses."

Joe Havens spat on the ground and scooped up his rifle. "Let's go get them back," he said grimly.

Bobby laughed sarcastically and shook his head. "They done pulled out."

"Well, why didn't you stop them?" Joe demanded.

Bobby drew deep on his cigarette, then spat in disgust. "How? I was over a half mile away. By the time I got down there, they was gone."

Joe looked ready to challenge the fact, then suddenly changed his mind, whirling to face Lester and Elmo. "This is all your fault!" he hissed.

"Joe, shut up," I said tiredly. I sat down on a log, taking off my hat and wadding it in my hands. "Question is, what do we do now?"

"Too far to go back to Whiskey City," Bobby said, crushing out his smoke. "On two horses and short of supplies, we'd never make it." He shot a long look at Lester and Elmo. "I don't suppose you got any supplies?"

Like a couple of whipped dogs, Lester and Elmo skulked back a step, scuffing their floppy boots in the dirt. "No," they said meekly.

"Well, that's just dandy!" Joe roared, smacking his fist into his palm. "Teddy, I swear, you shoulda let me kill them."

"Hey, lard can, it weren't our fault!" Elmo sputtered. "You fellers freighted away half the store. We figured once we caught up with you, you'd have plenty of grub."

"We had plenty," I quietly reminded them. "You boys fixed that."

"Yeah, well, you shoulda tied your horses better," Elmo shot back.

"Don't go trying to blame this on Teddy," Joe said, growling and taking a step toward Elmo.

Things were getting a bit out of hand, when Bobby's voice cut calmly through the din. "There's a town called Beaver Falls about thirty miles north of here," Bobby said. "I guess we best head there."

Well, sir, none of us wanted any part of that kind of a walk. I reckon if we'd put 'er to a vote, we'd all been in favor of throttling Lester and Elmo right then and there. But that wouldn't do us a lotta good, so I tried to think positive. "We could start now," I pointed out. "Them Russians, they might not go far, 'fore they stop again. We might still have a chance of running them down."

"Sounds good," Bobby said with a shrug.

"All right, Elmo, you and Lester go fetch your horses. We'll take turns riding," I decided.

"Now, just hold on a danged minute!" Elmo blustered. "Me and Lester never decided that we was gonna share our hosses with you."

Now, I'm a big man, and when I grabbed the front of Elmo's shirt, I snatched him clean off the ground. "I decided," I said with a growl, my face only inches from his.

"All right, all right," Elmo howled, his

arms and legs flapping like he thought he could fly. "No need to get so persnickety about it."

I set him down, not bothering at all to be gentle. "Go get them," I said, helping him along with a healthy shove.

Pulling at the seat of his britches, he glowered back over his shoulder at me, then finally jerked his head. "Come on, Lester," he mumbled, still tugging at his britches and muttering to himself as he led Lester away. "Dang big galoot. One of these days, I'm gonna . . ."

I suppose he had more to say, but by then, he'd wandered out of earshot. Grinding my teeth, I slapped my hat against my leg. Why couldn't anything ever be easy with them two? "What are you laughing at?" I demanded of Bobby, who was snickering up his sleeve.

"Danged if I know," he said, still chuckling as he shook his head. "But you gotta admit, there has to be something funny here. You should see your face."

Well, I was glad he was happy, 'cause we had one long walk ahead of us, and I didn't see anything good coming of it. As Lester and Elmo led their horses into camp, I took a deep breath and clapped my hat back on my head.

Joe promptly shoved Elmo aside and swung up on his horse. "I'm riding first," he announced.

I could spot another spat brewing, so I placed my arm around Elmo's shoulders and dragged him away. "It doesn't matter who walks first, we're all going to get our chance," I said.

Elmo didn't like it one bit, but for once he didn't start a row, and we set out without incident. We pushed hard, hustling right along, switching riders every so often. A couple hours shy of sunup, we just had to stop. We were beat, and them horses were staggering in their tracks.

We tended the horses, then collapsed in heaps on the ground. I reckon we were tired 'cause we slept well past daybreak. I was the first one up, feeling wicked as a witch. I'm a man that sets store by breakfast.

We weren't to have any, so I roused everybody and we set out. The horses were still mighty used up, so we all walked. We'd got off the trail a bit in the dark, and it took us a minute or two to pick it back up. Once we did, we didn't go two hundred yards before we found where the Russians had stopped.

His face turning so red I thought his hair would catch afire, Joe took off his hat, stomping in circles. "Five more minutes last night, and we woulda had them," he sputtered between clenched teeth.

I knew how he felt; my own jaw was locked tighter than a banker's hand around a dollar. Only Bobby seemed calm as he studied the trail. "They're starting to bear south," he said, looking down the trail after them. "Beaver Falls is a mite north of here."

"Two of us could take the horses and chase after them," I suggested, hating the thought of leaving the trail. Likely we'd never pick it back up again.

"Shoot, Teddy, them horses are used up," Joe said disgustedly. "We pushed them awful hard last night. They just ain't gonna stand any hard riding."

Bobby nodded, straightening up. "Face it, Teddy, we're gonna have to leave the trail and go into Beaver Falls for some supplies."

They were right, and I knew it. I just didn't like admitting it. Besides, I still saw one big problem: we were next to broke. "We haven't got more than a couple dollars between us. How do you plan to pay for horses and supplies?"

Well, no one had an answer to that one, but it never bothered Bobby Stamper none. He grinned and clapped me on the back. "We'll think of something when we get there."

Chapter Four

We rested ourselves and our two horses for the rest of the day, then set out bright and early the next day. Even so, we didn't make it to Beaver Falls by night, and were forced to make a dry camp, with nothing to eat.

We were a surly group, footsore and travel weary when we set out the next day. The thought of a hot meal and a cool drink that awaited us in Beaver Falls was all that kept us going. Just short of nightfall, we spotted the place.

Now, Bobby had said that Beaver Falls was a piddlin' little town out in the middle of nowhere, so we weren't expecting much. Boy, were we in for a shock. Beaver Falls was a piddlin' little place, but it was crammed to the rafters with folks.

They crowded the street, everyone gussied up in their Sunday best. I swear, I never saw so much hair oil in all my days. They all stared at us as we staggered into town on our last legs.

Ignoring them, we turned into the stable, which was the only place that wasn't packed—well, with people, anyway. The only two people in the barn were a burly, round-shouldered man and a big, rawboned kid with bad teeth and flaming red hair. No, sir, there weren't many folks in the barn, but it was jam-packed with horses. Looked to me like we'd have to butter our two skinny horses just to fit them in.

"Lively little place," I commented to Bobby as we went inside.

"Yeah," Bobby said, rubbing his chin. "I sure don't recollect there being this many folks in this burg. Sleepy little place as I recall."

"You've been here before?" I asked, an awful thought sneaking up on me as I remembered Bobby's previous occupation. "You didn't rob their bank?"

Bobby grinned, draping his arm over my

shoulder. "You know, I been thinking on that, and I can't rightly remember," he said, sounding mighty cheerful about it. "But I s'pect we'll find out soon enough."

Yeah, when some lawman collars us up, I thought sourly. The stable owner was shoeing a horse, but I didn't pay no mind to him, my eyes were on that pony. I let out a whistle; that horse was a beauty. A shiny red horse and standing a good eighteen hands high, that critter was the best horse I ever saw.

The hostler heard my whistle, dropping the hoof he was working on, to beam up at us. "Howdy, gents. Name's Cademus Mac-Galvin. I own this place. What can I do you fer?"

"You got room in here for two more horses?" I asked, tearing my eyes away from that horse.

"Always room for more," he assured me, looking at us curiously. "Two horses for five men? You boys is traveling mighty light, ain't you?" he ribbed with a hearty laugh, which withered and died real fast. "Costs two bits. Now, I don't mean to be insulting, but I reckon I better have it in advance. I mean, you folks look honest enough, but five men sharing two horses? Well, a body can't be too careful these days."

"You're surely right about that. Bobby, pay the man," I said, stepping past him to get a closer look at that sorrel horse. "We'll be in the market for some horses when we get ready to leave town. You got any for sale?" I asked, looking at that horse and doing some big dreaming.

"Not that one," the hostler said, hurriedly stepping between me and the sorrel. "That horse belongs to some fancy French feller. Goes by the name of Bordeaux," he said, pronouncing the name "Bardoo." "He's mighty proud of that animal. Treats it better than most fellers treat their wives."

"But you do have horses to sell?" Joe pressed.

"Sure, sure," the hostler said quickly. "When you boys get ready to leave town, come see me," he said, then shot a glance at that redheaded kid. "Fergus, move your sorry butt and tend these fellers' horses."

"Yes, Pa," the boy grumbled, leading our horses to the rear of the barn.

"Lots of folks in town," Bobby commented, looking out the door. "What's the big occasion?"

"This is trials week. Judge only comes once a year. Folks come from miles around to watch the trials and the hangings." The hostler grinned, rubbing his hands together. "This is my best time of the year," he said while the lad in the back snorted and rolled his eyes. "Don't get to see much of the trials, but I sure rake it in hand over fist."

"Never mind all the jawing," Lester bawled. "I'm 'bout starved to death. Let's find some place to get some grub."

"There's an eating house up the street a piece," the hostler commented. "Food's eatable if you're hungry, and there ain't been anyone get sick from eating there in almost a month."

That sounded good enough to me. I don't know about the others, but I was hungry enough to eat the south end of a north-bound mule. With me in the lead, we fought our way through the crowd up the street to the eating house. Now, if we thought the street was full of folks, it was nothing compared to that café. We had to stand inside the door for half an hour while the folks at the tables finished their chowing.

I was hungry, and I can't say that I liked the waiting, but I stood up to it better than Lester. I thought he was gonna have a conniption, 'specially when some frilled-up dude in a ruffled shirt lingered over his coffee.

"Hey, Mable, shake a leg!" Lester howled, kicking the fancy feller's chair.

"Yeah, fancy boy, we're powerful hungry," Elmo said, hooking his thumbs in his shell belt.

Now, that gent might have been purtied up like a dancehall girl, with lacy ruffles on his shirt, but from the mean look that sprang to his face, I could tell he was nobody to trifle with.

Fire blazing in his dark eyes, he rose slowly to his feet. He dabbed at his lips with a fancy handkerchief, then tossed it on the table with a quick, angry motion. "Monsieur, were you addressing me?" he asked, his tone dangerous.

"You dang right we was!" Elmo screeched, his face flaming red as his hand fell to his gun. All of a sudden, a puzzled look swept over his face. "Whadda you call me?" he sputtered. Scratching his head, he glanced around the room."What did that tinhorn call me?"

Lester dug a finger in his ear, cocking his head off to the side. "Uh, I ain't real sure, but I think he called you Missy something or another."

"What the devil does that mean?" Elmo demanded belligerently. He glanced back at

Bobby, Joe and me. "Is that something I can kill him fer?"

To this day, I don't know why I did it. By rights, I shoulda let Elmo take his medicine. I mean, I could see that fancy little dude was gonna twist Elmo's tail, and he sure enough had it coming. But for some reason, I grabbed the two brothers by the shoulders, hauling them back. "Don't pay no mind to them, mister. We've been traveling several days short of grub. I reckon we're just hungry," I said.

"That's no excuse for bad manners and filthy appearances," the man said, and despite the funny way he talked, his highfalutin manner came right through.

By now, I wanted to swat him once myself, but that wouldn't do us a bit of good, so I forced a smile on my face. "Yes, sir, you're right about that, and we're terribly sorry," I said. "Now, if you'll excuse us, I see an empty table over yonder."

For a second, I thought the dude would put up a scrap, but with a little flip of his wrist, he let us pass. Elmo wanted to stay and jaw, but I kept pushing him in the back until we reached the table. Elmo jerked away from me, his face still redder than a sunset. "Now, why in tarnation did you go and do that for?" he growled.

"Yeah," Joe put in sourly. "I was all primed to see a scrap."

"We ain't got time for that," I said.

"From now on, just keep your snoot outta my business," Elmo said. "I won't stand for no butting in."

"Be glad he did," Bobby said, cheerfully slapping Elmo on the back. "Take it from me, that gent was bad news," he added as he slid into a chair.

That settled Elmo down, but as the waitress came to our table, he continued to glare at that fancy feller. That waitress didn't bother asking what we wanted. She just carted over five bowls of stew and a platter of cornbread.

We were all hungry and took to that grub like a fish to water, but Lester really dug in. He lifted that bowl to his lips and shoveled stew into his mouth like a man pitching straw. In less than a shake, he finished that bowl, and three hunks of cornbread.

"Man, that was good!" he said, belching loudly and smacking his lips. "I think I'll go see if they got any more."

Toting his bowl, he strutted up to the long counter at the front of the café, squeezing in between two cowhands. Smiling, the waitress refilled his bowl, then handed it back.

"Say, ma'am, you reckon I could get a few more slabs of that cornbread?" I heard him ask.

"Certainly," the waitress said, plopping a couple of chunks on top of his bowl.

"Hey, guys! Look what I got!" Lester shouted, whirling around to show us. As he turned, he bumped right into that fancy feller, who had finally finished his coffee and gotten around to leaving.

When they ran together, Lester dumped his bowl all down the front of that ruffled shirt. A stricken look on his face, Lester stumbled back a step. "Gee, mister, I'm plumb sorry about that," he mumbled as cold fury swept over that fancy-pants' face.

"Idiot!" he screamed.

"No need to get riled, a little lye soap and some scrubbing will take—"

Lester never got a chance to finish. With a chopping blow, ol' fancy-drawers knocked him to the floor. As Lester lay in the spilt soup, fancy-pants held his hand out behind him. A buttoned-down gent with him pulled out a long-barreled pistol and passed it forward to fancy-pants.

Very coldly, that fancy dude aimed the pistol down at Lester.

Chapter Five

Jack Warren leaned his chair back against the wall of the saloon, enjoying the cool breeze that blew down the street. At ease with his world, Jack Warren puffed on a cigar, occasionally taking a pull from the bottle that stood on the boardwalk beside his chair.

For three days, Jack Warren had waited outside the saloon in Miller's Landing, a small town in northern Utah. Warren didn't like waiting, but for the money involved, he would wait for as long as it took.

Jack was dusting the ash from his cigar when he first saw them. They came into sight suddenly, rounding the corner of the general store, which was the last building on the street. Even from a distance, Jack Warren knew these were the men he waited for.

Warren drew deep on his cigar, studying the men closely as they rode slowly toward him. Dressed in suits, they might appear at first glance as soft tenderfeet, but Jack knew these were hard, desperate men.

Grim-faced, the three men rode slowly up the street, looking neither left nor right, a string of spare mounts trailing behind them. One man carried a carpetbag tied to his saddle horn, his hand resting on the bag.

As they came closer, Jack sat his chair legs on the boardwalk, rising gracefully to his feet. Now he could see that one of the men sat in the saddle funny, clinging to the horn like he'd been hurt.

"You Fedarov?" Jack called softly.

Like wolves, the three men turned to look at Jack. The injured man grimaced and straightened in the saddle. "I am Boris Fedarov; you are Warren?"

Warren nodded. "You bring the money?"

"Yes," Fedarov said, sliding stiffly from his horse. "We may have another job for you."

"Let's go inside and talk it over," Warren invited, tossing his cigar into the street. He scooped up the bottle, motioning with his head for the three Russians to follow him inside. As they stepped inside the cool interior of the saloon, Jack whistled to the boy who ran errands for the saloonkeeper. Jack tossed two silver dollars to the boy, then jerked his thumb in the direction of the street. "There's a bunch of horses in the street. Take them down to the stable and see they're tended to."

"Yes, sir," the boy said, grinning up at Jack as he clutched the money in his fist.

At this hour in the afternoon, the saloon was empty. Even the bartender was in the back, perfecting his own brew of whiskey. Jack took four glasses from the bar, then led his companions to a table in the back corner.

"Looks like you boys ran into some trouble," Jack commented, pouring the glasses full.

Vanya Drago ignored the comment, his blocky face hard as he leaned across the table. "Your brothers are prepared to do the job we discussed?" he demanded.

Warren smiled over the top of his glass. "They're on their way to Frisco right now. Soon as you pay me the money, I'll send word to them. If that czar, shows up, he's a dead man."

"It is agreed? We pay part now, and the rest once the czar is dead?" Dmitri asked.

"That's what the plan was," Warren agreed with an offhand shrug.

"Very good," Fedarov said, nodding to Vanya, who had carried the carpetbag inside with him.

"You mentioned something about another job?" Warren asked, licking his lips as Vanya counted out the money.

"Yes," Dmitri replied. "There are some men following us. They have already attacked us once."

"You want me to slow them down," Warren replied, a slow grin spreading across his face.

"No!" Fedarov said, slamming his fist down on the table. "We want you to kill them!"

I sprang from my seat, bounding across the room in four big steps. Chopping down with my big fist, I whacked that pistol from his hand. The gun skitted across the floor, and Bobby, who was right behind me, scooped it up.

"A little spilt soup ain't worth killing a man for," I said, hoping that fancy gent would see reason.

Well, he never done it. The hate that blazed in his eyes shocked me and rocked me back on my heels.

"Monsieur, you act foolishly," the buttoned-down hombre said. "Do you not know who this is? This is Count Paul Bordeaux. You are most foolish to provoke his ire."

"I've been foolish before," I replied with a shrug. "But I am sorry."

"You have insulted my honor!" Bordeaux shouted, holding his hand out to the gent behind him. "I demand satisfaction!" he said as his helper placed a pair of gloves in his hand.

Now, I figured he was gonna yank on them gloves and we was gonna duke it out. Well, that weren't what he had in mind. He snapped up straight, clicking his heels together. "My honor demands satisfaction!" he said, then whacked me across the mouth with them gloves.

Now, that was the last thing I'd been expecting. While he didn't hurt me none, them gloves in the whiskers did sting a mite. The short of the story is that I just rared back and lowered the jack on him. Without even thinking, I swatted him right on the snoot.

It weren't near my best punch, but it did the trick. He skidded across the floor on the seat of his britches, crashing into a table and knocking it over. He came up mighty fast, I'll give him that. Covered with gruel and grog, his nose leaking blood, he glared at me like he wished harm to fall on my head. I swear, he was putting off heat like a Franklin stove. He straightened his short-tailed jacket with a quick jerk, then pointed a finger at me. "I shall kill you for that!" he hissed.

He was serious, a blind man could see that. 'Course, if he expected to scare me to death, he was in for a foolin'. I mean, it seemed like here lately, somebody was always trying to salt my hide. Whoever this Paul Bordeaux was, I figured I could handle whatever he brought.

No, sir, he never scared me, but we had more than enough trouble, and I figured it best to try and smooth his feathers. "No need to get all het up," I said, spreading my hands in front of me. "This here was just an accident. Ain't no need in anybody getting killed over it."

Standing very straight, he threw back his shoulders. Despite the fact that he had slop all over his shirt, and a bean mashed on his forehead, he looked right stately. "Tomorrow at noon, you shall meet me outside of town," he said, then marched out of the room.

That buttoned-down gent squirmed, shifting his feet and wringing his feet. Seemed like he wanted to say something, but then he just took the count's pistol from Bobby and hurried after his friend.

Bobby shook his head, chuckling as he patted me on the back. "Well, Teddy, I gotta say, you sure know how to make friends, but if you're done socializing, let's get down to business."

"You got any ideas?" I asked as Joe and Elmo hauled a groggy Lester to his feet.

"Not yet," Bobby admitted and somehow managed to sound cheerful about it. "But I would say you're gonna have to kill that man," he said, turning serious, his eyes trailing to the door where Bordeaux just left. "Or he's gonna kill you."

Jack Warren poured another drink while he studied the three Russians seated across the table from him. "How many men do you want killed?" he asked, fishing in his pocket for another cigar.

"We are not sure," Dmitri Grazovitch replied. "The extra horses we had are theirs, so there is at least three, probably not more than six. When we captured the horses, we didn't have time to get an accurate count on their numbers," he added, neglecting to mention that it was pure luck that they had the horses.

Warren frowned, pulling the unlit cigar from his mouth. "They are afoot, then?"

"Yes, or at most, they have one or two mounts," Drago answered.

"Where was you, when you boys swiped their horses?"

"I do not know exactly. Two days' travel behind us," Fedarov said.

Warren lit his cigar, smiling as he waved out the match. "Beaver Falls. They'll head to Beaver Falls for fresh horses. I can pick up their trail there."

"How long will this take?" Drago asked.

"Take me a day to round up enough men for the job, and it's close to two days' travel back to Beaver Falls. After that? It depends on how long it takes me to find out who they are and where they went."

Grazovitch smiled. "Perhaps we can help you with that." Grazovitch glanced over at his friends. "Mikhail is in Beaver Falls."

"Who?" Warren grunted.

"An associate of ours," Grazovitch answered. "He was waiting in Beaver Falls, in case we missed the duchess at Whiskey City." He glanced quickly at Warren. "Is there any way to get a message to him?"

Warren looked up and scratched his neck. "No telegraph in Beaver Falls," he said, then smiled. "Mail rider's in town. He'll be leaving at first light, and he goes right through Beaver Falls. You could send a letter with him."

"Excellent," Fedarov said, the pain of his wounds suddenly forgotten. "We shall contact Mikhail. He will find the men you seek and point them out to you once you reach Beaver Falls. All you will have to do is kill them."

Warren took the cigar from his mouth and dropped it carelessly on the table. Warren reached for the money, but Drago slammed his hand down on the pile. "We do not pay for excuses or failure," he warned.

"Then there is nothing to worry about," Warren said easily. "Those men are as good as dead!"

Chapter Six

The next day we hung around town, spending most of our time in the saloon out of the sun. While the others spent their time dreaming up ways to make the money we needed, I kept an eye out for Bordeaux. I didn't want to kill him, and I 'specially didn't want him killing me. So far, I'd managed to duck him, but I knew if we didn't get out of town fast, he'd catch up to me.

Bobby was in hog heaven. Trying to come up with a fast way to raise a lot of money was right up his alley. He'd come up with some doozy schemes, but so far they were all way too wild.

Tired of sitting in the saloon, I left Bobby to his scheming and went outside for some fresh air. Now, usually, I'd rather rassle a bear in a barrel than take a walk, but tonight I was in a wandering mood.

I meandered along the street, looking in the shops and at the houses, without really seeing them. Liking the feel of the cool breeze against my face, I stopped at the edge of town, looking out at a big revival tent that had gone up earlier that day. I stared at the tent, listening to the singing, hoping for some inspiration. Whoever was singing, well, she had the voice of an angel. It made my heart glad just to hear it. After a bit, the singing stopped and some fire and brimstone preacher took over.

I listened for a minute, then started to turn away. All that yelling and damnation wasn't my style of preaching. I took to preachers that talked about the forgiveness of the Lord. That's when I first saw her. I was just fixing to head back to join my friends, when she came out of the tent.

Now, there's some people in the world who once you get shut off them, you hope never to see them again, and Lilly Simmons was sure enough one of them. I had prayed never to see her again.

Not that she wasn't nice to look at. I reckon she was pretty as a mountain sunrise, but she was also trouble. Lilly Simmons was like lightning, pretty to look at from a safe distance, but just getting close to her was enough to make your skin prickle and your hair stand on end. And just like lightning, if she ever touched you, your hash was fried.

I eased back in the shadows, hoping that if she saw me, she wouldn't recognize me. I mean, I seen that woman twice in my life, and both times, she done her dangdest to get me killed. The fact that I was still sucking in air wasn't from a lack of trying on her part.

Last time I saw her, she was fleeing into a blizzard and cursing my soul. At the time, I'd hoped never to see her again.

Holding a frilly little umbrella, she came right at me. Now, to give the devil her due, Miss Lilly had a way of walking that put butterflies in a man's belly. I tell you, it was hard not to stare, but as she drew near, I tore my eyes away. Looking down at the ground, I jerked my hat down a notch lower. I was just hoping she wouldn't recognize me, but I don't have that kind of luck.

She came by so close that I coulda touched her. As the smell of her fancy perfume filled my nostrils, my hand fingers tickled the butt of my shooter. I didn't know what she might try to do if she saw me, but shooting me or sticking me with a knife wasn't out of the question. I did know that with her around, I felt a heap safer with my hand on my gun.

She took one step past me and my knees were going slack with relief, when she stopped. My shoulders humped and a groan rolled past my lips. "Teddy?" she said and started to turn. "Teddy Cooper, is that you?"

I swear, it was like rounding the corner on a narrow trail and finding yourself face-to-face with a catamount. You knew you were about to get your backside mauled, and there wasn't a danged thing you could do about it. "Yeah, it's me," I grunted, ready to throw up my hands and defend myself.

I nearly had a stroke when she smiled and jumped at me. No, she didn't try to snuff me, she done the last thing I expected; she threw her arms around me and gave me a feathery kiss on the cheek. "My word, it's so good to see you again!" she exclaimed and danged if she didn't sound like she meant it. "What ever brings you to Beaver Falls?"

"We're on our way to California," I blurted out.

"You're leaving Whiskey City, then?"

"No," I said slowly, mind whirling like a prairie twister. "We're on our way out there to do a favor for a friend."

She laughed, patting my arm. "That sounds so much like you, always helping others." All of a sudden, the merry look drained off her face, and she turned serious. She reached up and straightened my collar and smoothed the front of my shirt. "That's an admirable quality, Teddy. You've turned into quite a young man, and you should be proud of yourself."

Now, I didn't have the foggiest idea what to say. She sounded sincere, but I knew that woman could be sweet as rock candy when the notion struck her. Still, her compliment embarrassed me, and I felt my face burn as I watched my worn boots scuffle in the dirt. "Why, thank you, ma'am," I heard myself mumble.

She laughed again, taking my hand in hers. "I can see that I have embarrassed you. I'm sorry," she said cheerfully. "You mentioned that you weren't alone. Is Eddy with you? Did you ever marry that sweet girl?"

"Not yet, but we're fixing to, soon as we get the time."

"You should make time. Eddy is a lovely young lady," Lilly scolded mildly. "I take that she isn't with you on this trip?"

"No, she's coming along behind," I replied, feeling like I'd dunked my head in a vat of honey. For an ol' gal who offered ten grand to anyone who snuffed me, and tried her dangdest to do the job herself, Lilly was yakking with me like we were long-lost pals. 'Fore I knew it, I was talking to her the same way. "Bobby and Joe Havens came with me," I said, then added sourly, "And Elmo and Lester too."

Lilly snickered, covering her mouth with a hand shoved down in a lacy glove. "Lester and Elmo, they're so funny."

"They're a royal pain in the backside!" I growled. "I shoulda let you kill them."

Well, I hadn't meant to say that, but somehow it sorta blurted out. I mean it was true, she had been ready to kill them two numbskull brothers. She'd been hoping to get her hands on the mine Turley gave to me, and she'd been more than ready to wax Lester and Elmo to get her hands on that mine. Well, the short of the story is, I stopped her. Sometimes, shoot, most times, I rued that day.

Anyway, when I brought it up, a look of pain rolled across her face. She squeezed my hand and cast her eyes down. "I've caused you a lot of trouble. It's a wonder you don't hate me," she said, her voice so soft I could barely hear it. "Please forgive me," she pleaded, and danged if she didn't sound sincere. She shook her head. "I wish I could take it all back." She raised her head and I could see the redness in her eyes and the twin tears tracking down her cheeks. "Can you possibly find it in your heart to forgive me?"

All right, maybe I'm a sucker, a bigger sap than a redwood, but I just couldn't look into those teary eyes and be mean. It just wasn't in me. Now, I still had a nagging doubt about her in the back of my mind, but I pushed it aside and nodded. "Reckon everybody deserves a second chance," I mumbled, twisting my hat in my hands.

"Thank you," she breathed, giving my hand a little squeeze. "If there was anyone in the world I wanted to forgive me and know that I've changed, it was you."

Well, what do you say to that? I surely didn't know. All I could do was hem and haw, mashing my hat some more. "Where's Bobby and Mr. Havens? I would love to see them," Lilly said, then added, almost as an afterthought, "and Elmo and Lester as well."

Well, my doubts about her sprang back in full force. She had to be lying now. Nobody ever wanted to see them two. "They're all over at the saloon. I reckon they'll be wanting to see you too." I figured that was the truth.

I figured them boys would want to have a word with her. 'Course, it might not be the words she wanted to hear.

Holding that frilly little rain bonnet in her left hand, she slipped her right arm inside of mine. She asked a jillion questions as we strolled up the street toward the saloon. For an old gal who'd only been in Whiskey City twice, she sure knew a lot about the place. She asked about Turley, Iris and Gid, even Mr. Burdett, and she seemed to be really interested.

I was just telling her about Iris and Gid getting themselves hitched when we stepped into the saloon. For a second, the whole place seemed to stop in its tracks. I mean, just for an instant, the place looked like a painting I saw one time. No one moved; the bunch of them just stared at Miss Lilly.

I reckon every man in the joint was gaping at her, but I was watching my friends. To a man, they all looked like they'd just had their jaws jacked. With open mouths and wide eyes, they stared at us.

Elmo was the first to recover. His face white as a wagon cover, he shoved back his chair. Stabbing a quivering finger at her, he sprang to his feet. "You!" he sputtered, saliva dribbling down his chin.

"Hello, Elmo," Lilly replied graciously as she glided gracefully across the room.

Elmo swallowed hard, then wiped his mouth on the back of his hand. He started to draw his gun, then stopped, plumb out of options. "What do you want?" he demanded, a note of fear in his voice.

"I just wished to say hello," Lilly replied, smiling sweetly. "How are you gentlemen?"

An awkward silence began to build that grated on my nerves. I was tracking down something to say, when Lilly took matters into her own hands. "I trust I wouldn't be disturbing you gentlemen if I sat down?" she asked.

His face hard, Bobby motioned to an empty chair with a flip of his hand. "Help yourself," he said.

Didn't look like anyone was gonna do the right thing, so I reached around her and dragged a chair back for her. Lilly flashed me a smile as she slid into her chair. "Thank you, Teddy," she said, then glanced across the table. "Teddy tells me that you are headed to California."

"That's right! What's it to you?" Elmo screeched, he and Lester edging away.

"Nothing really," Lilly replied with an offhand shrug. "It's just so nice to see you again.

I just wish we had more time to visit. Teddy said you were going to help a friend, so I imagine you'll be leaving in the morning."

"Fat chance of that!" Joe Havens growled, disgustedly slamming his glass down on the table.

Lilly's eyebrows shot up a fraction. "You have troubles?"

"You might say that," Bobby conceded, rubbing his chin as he leaned back in his chair.

"Anything I can help you with?" Lilly asked, then hastily added, "I mean, I feel as if I owe you all."

Lester cringed back in his chair, swallowing so hard, I could hear it from where I sat. "Owe us what?" he squawked in a hushed voice. "What are you gonna do to us?" he asked in a worried tone, hitching his chair away, then yelping as Lilly patted his hand.

"I know I've caused you a lot of grief in the past, and I am truly sorry. If there is any way I can help, I would like to." Her voice was soft as she batted her lovely green eyes at us. "I would like to make amends."

Now, I figured that was a mighty sweet and generous offer, but the others, they didn't see it thataway. "Unless you can get your hands on four horses and a raft of supplies, there ain't a lot you can do," Joe Havens said disgustedly.

"You don't happen to have four extra horses, do you, Lilly?" Bobby asked, and as Lilly slowly shook her head, I could hear the jeering note in Bobby's laugh. "Then I don't see how you can help us," he said, pushing back his chair. "I can't say it's been a pleasure.

As Bobby left, Lester and Elmo scurried after him, edging around the table and giving Lilly a wide berth. Joe stood up, and I had the feeling he was gonna say something, but then he just snatched up the bottle and hurried after the others.

Feeling like we'd been rude, I hesitated. "I'm real sorry about that, Miss Lilly," I said, my eyes following my friends.

"It's okay, Teddy," Lilly said, but her tone didn't make it sound okay. "I can't really blame them. Not everyone can forgive as easily as you."

All of a sudden, I felt kinda special. "Thank you," I said, and shot a hard glance at the door. "I guess I better go catch them. Don't worry, I'll talk to them, they'll come around," I promised, wanting to do something for her. As I hustled to catch up with my friends, I promised myself that I would do something for her.

As I sauntered out of the saloon, my friends were waiting on the boardwalk. "Where'd you bump into her?" Bobby asked, his fingers working smoothly as he rolled a smoke.

"She's singing out at the revival tent," I answered, giving the whole group a stern frown. "You fellers coulda been a little nicer to her," I accused.

"You forgetting that she tried to kill us, not so awful long ago?" Bobby asked, an amused smirk on his face.

"She said she's real sorry about that," I protested. "She said she's changed."

Bobby snorted, flicking his cigarette into the street. "Yeah, and the sun is going to come up in the west tomorrow," he growled. "I'm going to find a place to bed down. You fellers coming?"

"Yeah, I guess so," I mumbled.

"You guys go on ahead," Joe Havens said, waving a hand at us. "I think I'll do a little nosing around. Maybe I'll bump into somebody I know, hopefully somebody who owes me."

I smiled to myself as the others started away. For a feller who always acted gruff and cantankerous, I knew Joe had a soft streak way deep inside. Now, I'd known Joe Havens my life long, but it was just since I took over this sheriffing job that I really saw him. I'd noticed that whenever some poor soul down on his luck drifted into Joe's saloon, he never left with an empty belly. Joe might gripe the whole time, but he always anted up a free meal and a snort of whiskey. And though I didn't know for sure, I had a suspicion that they also left with a little change jingling in their pockets.

Another thing I'd noticed was that whenever a body around town needed a helping hand, Joe was always there. Joe might gripe and act surly as a bear, but he did his share.

Just like now. I needed help, and Joe was here. True, he'd spent most of his time criticizing and bellyaching, but he never once mentioned quitting on us and going home. And he wouldn't, neither.

Smiling, I patted him on the shoulder. "You watch yourself," I cautioned.

"Who are you, my mammy?" Joe snorted, shoving my hand away. "Teddy, I swear, you worry like an old widder woman. Why, I was wiping my own nose 'fore you were born."

I chuckled and shook my head. "Just be careful," I warned, turning to catch up with the others.

"Teddy, hold up a second," Joe said, his voice soft as he grabbed my arm. "Look, I know I ain't your pappy, and maybe it ain't my place to say," he said, then hesitated. He dropped his hand from my arm, looking absently down the street. "What I'm trying to say is, you play it close to the vest around that Lilly woman. I don't trust her none." Joe awkwardly squeezed my arm, then lightly punched my shoulder. "I reckon I like you, boy, and I wouldn't want to see you get in trouble. Take my word for it, that woman is poison mean and she ain't about to change."

Five men rode into Beaver Falls. Like so many ghosts, they materialized slowly as they rode out of the darkness and into the lights of the town. Their horses were covered with dust, and their faces were drawn and haggard. Despite the long ride behind them, the men rode alert, with hands on guns, and hard, watchful eyes. They left their horses with Fergus at the stable, paying cash for their care.

Their spurs jingled softly as they walked down the boardwalk toward the saloon. As they passed the small gap between the hotel and the general store, a soft whisper called out to them from the shadows. "Are you Jack Warren?"

The leader of the group stopped, peering into the darkness. "I am," he said, his hand resting on the butt of his pistol. "You'd be Mikhail?"

"Yes. The men you seek are here."

After Teddy left, Lilly lingered at the table, her thoughts whirling as she stared at the scarred tabletop. Somehow, she had to win the confidence of the men from Whiskey City. So much depended on it!

Lilly smiled to herself as she reached for her umbrella. The one gift she had was manipulating men, and these backwater clods from the hills should be easy. Ignoring the stares directed her way, Lilly walked coolly from the bar.

The street was deserted, and Lilly could hear the faint sound of singing drifting up from the revival meeting just outside of town. Liking the clean, crisp feel to the night, Lilly walked slowly to the hotel.

The dim hallway was deserted as she unlocked her door. Dropping the key into her clutch, she stepped inside, feeling for a match. Her hands were probing the darkness for the lamp on the table, when a heavily accented voice broke the silence. "They are here."

Lilly jumped, a squeal of surprise escaping past her lips. "Sergei, how did you get in here?" she demanded, placing a hand over her suddenly racing heart.

The man laughed, almost soundlessly. "It wasn't so hard," he said, crossing the room to stand close to her. "They are here. You can handle the job?"

Lilly twisted her hands together, staring up at his face. This man frightened her. From the faint moonlight drifting in the window, she could barely make out the hard outline of his hawklike face. "Of course," she said slowly. "Do not worry about a thing. They are men, I can handle them."

She heard the soft chuckle and felt the roughness of his knuckles as he caressed her cheek. "I hope so," he said softly. "We do not accept failure."

Chapter Seven

Jack Warren woke his men up early. They had spent the night in a long low tent, set up on the other side of town from the revival tent. They'd paid a quarter for a cot and cheap blanket, and were lucky to get that. They shared the tent with twenty other men, and as many slept just outside on the ground.

Warren pulled a cot into a corner, then called his men over. He looked to make sure, but the rest of the men in the tent were sleeping. Most of the sleeping men stumbled into the tent well after two in the morning. They wouldn't be rolling out of their bunks for hours.

"There's gonna be a duel today," Warren said, keeping his voice down to a whisper.

"That Frenchman Bordeaux's gonna jump that Cooper feller in the street this morning."

"How do you know that?" the man known as Sid asked.

Warren smiled and held up a slip of paper. "Our friend sent word to me," he said. "Now, Nelson, I want you on the roof of the hotel, and Hank, I want you in the loft of the barn. When the shooting starts, make sure that Cooper don't walk away from the fight."

As Jack Warren and his men trooped off to find something to eat, a man several cots away sat up. Despite the fact that he had been fast asleep only minutes earlier, the man was alert. His eyes bright and hard, he rubbed his chin thoughtfully.

A look of determination springing to his wide face, Joe Havens swung his feet over the edge of the cot and stood up. These men meant to kill Teddy!

Wanting to learn more about the men and who hired them, Joe slipped quietly from the tent. Keeping his distance, Joe followed the men up the street, watching intently as they entered the café.

Leaning against the corner of the street, Joe paused. He wanted to keep an eye on these men, but he had to warn Teddy. His mind made up, Joe cut between two build-

ings, making haste for the flat just outside of
town where he knew his friends were sleeping.

Normally a cautious man, Joe Havens was
excited and in a hurry now. He didn't pay as
much attention as he should have. He didn't
notice the figure watching him from a second-
story window in the hotel. He didn't even notice as the figure hurried out of the back door
of the hotel, following Joe through the gray
light of the early morning.

That morning, I rolled outta my blankets,
feeling stiff as a rusty pump and sour as cactus berries. The place where I'd lain down
was lumpy and proved to be uneven as a ca-
mel's back. I was sore as a mashed thumb;
'course, all that walking hadn't helped either.

I dearly wanted a cup of coffee, but I knew,
without checking, that my pockets were dry
as an Arizona homestead. Rolling my shoulders to loosen them up, I studied on a way to
get a cup.

I was just about to give up on the notion
when I spotted a fancied-up wagon parked
next to that revival tent. What's more than
that, at the back of the wagon, I saw a feller
stoking a small fire. Even as I watched, he

took a pot from the coals and poured himself a cup.

Now, I reckoned if I was to mosey over there, he might just offer me a cup of that coffee. I didn't feel easy about what I was fixin' to do; fact is, I felt like a stray dog, mooching and begging, but I was gonna do it anyway. After all, I couldn't see no harm in a free cup of coffee. Boy, was I wrong.

But I didn't know that then, and I was already lumbering stiffly up to his fire. "Howdy," I called, trying to sound cheerful.

The man spun around, his face hard. "What do you want?" he asked, a note of suspicion in his tone.

I shrugged, licking my lips and staring enviously at that cup in his hand. "I was just out stretching my legs and saw your fire, thought I'd swing by and say howdy," I said, too embarrassed to come right out and say why I was really here. "My name is Teddy Cooper, by the way."

He was gonna have to shift that cup from his right hand to his left to take my hand, and for a second I didn't think he would do it. Finally, he nodded, shifting the cup and grasping my hand in a limp grasp. "Richard Philander. Reverend Richard Philander."

"Preachin' man, huh?" I said with a grunt,

thinking he didn't look nor act like any preacher I ever saw. He didn't bother answering, he just took another slurp from that cup. My mouth fairly watering, I tried to fire up a conversation. "This must be your revival tent then?"

"Yes," he replied. "We have been spreading the word among the uncivilized tribes. It is our calling to bring Christianity to the West."

Now, for a gospel man, Reverend Richard Philander wasn't a very cheery cuss, nor very charitable, neither. Why, I'd been standing here a minute and he hadn't bothered to offer me a cup yet. It didn't appear like he had a mind to either, but I wanted a taste of that coffee powerful bad, and wasn't ready to give up just yet.

"That's a mighty fine thing you are doing. Bringing preaching to all those folks," I commented, hoping a compliment might jar him loose. "Yes, sir, that's a mighty fine thing to do."

"I've felt the calling," he informed me, then looked me up and down. "I don't recall seeing you at the meeting last night. You are a Christian?"

"Yes, sir," I said immediately.

"Good," Reverend Philander replied, finally starting to thaw a mite. "Since you didn't get a chance to donate to the cause last night, perhaps you might like to make a contribution on this glorious morning?" As he finished his speech, a greasy smile slid onto his face, and his hand poked out, palm up.

I frowned; this wasn't going at all like I figured. Shuffling my feet, I glanced down at his hand, then back up at his face. "I surely would like to, Reverend, but you see—"

His hand snaked out another inch closer to me as he cut me off. "Now, Mr. Cooper, I can surely see that you are a fine, upstanding Christian man. Surely, you can see that it is your duty to help bring word of the Lord to this land?"

"Yes, sir, I do," I agreed, edging back a step. I wanted to get some breathing room between us, but Philander pressed after me, his hand out front like some kind of divining rod.

I tell you, I was ready to break and run like a schoolboy, when I heard a call from behind me. "Teddy, I wondered where the devil you wandered off to," Bobby Stamper called as he loped up to the fire.

Now, when it came to gall, Bobby Stamper ranks right up there with the best of them. He took one look at that pot on the fire and broke into a big grin. "Say, is that coffee I smell?" he asked loudly as he crossed to the fire. "You don't mind if I help myself to a cup?" he asked, already picking up the pot.

Philander didn't look like he cared sharing, but he nodded grudgingly. "Teddy, you want a cup?" Bobby asked as he poured himself a cup.

I nodded heartily, feeling like I'd just been pulled from a snake den. After Bobby poured our cups full, we stood in silence, savoring our coffee. The silence didn't last long. I reckon Philander had finally got good and woke up, and had a full head of wind in his sails.

"As I was telling your friend here," he started, and as he paused, I saw him look Bobby up and down, trying to estimate how deep his pockets were, I reckon. "We bring comfort and spirituality to the pioneers of this land, but as you can well guess, it takes a lot of money to keep such a ministry going. For not only do we bring the gospel, we provide food, clothing, and medicine."

As he spoke, that syrupy smile crept back on his face, and the reverend's hand began to inch out again. He puffed up his chest and strutted around the fire. "This ministry has brought the word to the gold towns of Colorado and Nevada. We've ministered in the cow camps of Texas. We brought aid and comfort to the farmers of Nebraska after drought wiped out their crops."

As Philander droned on and on, Bobby shot a smirk my way and cut his eyes up at the sky. I thought he would laugh out loud as the reverend told of how he brought food and medicine to the victims of a smallpox epidemic in Kansas.

"Boy, Reverend, you're a heckuva feller," Bobby exclaimed.

The reverend tried to conceal it, but he just couldn't keep the cabbage-eating grin off his face. "We do the best we can," he acknowledged, then hung his head a mite. "But as I was explaining to your friend, the cost is terrible. We are always short of funds. I thought you boys might like to make a contribution. Helping others is the best way to cleanse your own soul."

Right then, I felt like a treed coon, and wanted to skedaddle outta there, but Bobby seemed perfectly at ease. I mean, I've met a few of the preachers who travel from town to town, and better men you'll never find. 'Course, there's a rotten apple in every barrel, and Philander smelled wormy as a fishhook to me.

To begin with, for a man who was claiming

to be poor as a salt flat cow, Philander looked mighty well-heeled to me. He had on a fancy suit, and a ring on nigh every finger, and a couple of them rings were big enough to choke a donkey. I hadn't missed that hideout gun, tucked under his left arm. I hate to say it of a man claiming to be a man of God, but Reverend Philander had a seedy, shiftless look to him.

I drained my coffee and wanted to vamoose, but that danged Bobby was in a talking mood. Now, when Bobby gets to talking with that devilish grin on his face and a shining in his eyes, I know he's baiting someone. Trouble is, usually when they get enough, it's always me caught in the middle.

I had doubts aplenty, but Bobby had none. He smiled and clapped the reverend on the back. "You know, preacher, I'd be more than honored to kick some jack into your kitty."

Reverend Philander licked his lips, and all of a sudden his eyes got all beady. "That's wonderful!" he shouted, rubbing his hands together. "How much were you thinking of contributing? I must remind you how dire the need is. When we leave here, we are traveling to southern Utah, where a whole town was wiped out by a flood. It'll take a lot of money to help get those kind folks back on their feet again."

"A flood!" Bobby howled, covering his mouth with his hand. "I hadn't heard of that. Did you, Teddy?"

Now, I had no idea what the crazy devil was up to this time, but against my better judgment, I decided to play along. "No, sir, I hadn't heard tell of that. Why, that is just awful."

"A ghastly thing," the Reverend Richard Philander assured us, his tone somber as a hanging judge. "Whole families uprooted, houses washed away, but that isn't the worst of it." The reverend hung his head. "Hungry, crying children sleeping in the mud," he moaned, shaking his head sadly. "As you can well imagine, sickness is upon them. They need food, medicine, and dry blankets."

Bobby rubbed his chin, looking somber all of a sudden. "Why, that's just terrible," he said as Philander's hand began to crawl out again.

"Then you will help these unfortunate souls?"

"You bet we will!" Bobby said, smacking his fist in his palm. "The thing is, we've had a bit of bad luck ourselves."

For a second, Philander didn't want to believe it. I could tell that he wasn't happy about wasting twenty minutes of his best bull snorting on us, but he wasn't ready to call in his dogs. He glanced at me and I nodded sadly as the preacher's hand wilted back down to his side. "I'm sorry to hear of your troubles," he said, his face pinched up like a man who just swallered a dose of castor oil.

"Yes, sir, we was robbed by a bunch of dastardly thieves," Bobby said, snatching the reverend's hand. "But don't you fret none, me and Teddy, we aim to do our share," Bobby said, and commenced to digging in his pockets. "Let's divvy up, Teddy."

Now, by then, I done decided that Bobby was plumb addled, but I mined out my pockets. I didn't have more than a couple of cents, but Bobby took it and added it with his own. Between us, we didn't have more than a half dollar, but the way Bobby worried it around in his hand, you'd thought it was a fortune. Finally, he scraped half of it off into Philander's hand. "It ain't much, but I reckon every little bit helps. I wish we could do more." Bobby finished his coffee, sat the cup down, and started to turn away, then stopped suddenly. "Say!" You said them folks were needing blankets? Well, We got some blankets, I reckon we could spare a couple."

My chin slapped me full in the chest. What the devil was he up to? We didn't have one blanket. I was still trying to figure out what was going on, when Philander hastily interrupted. "Oh, no, I couldn't possibly accept them. You men have done more than enough," he said, herding us in the direction of town. "I wouldn't dream of taking your blankets. Do not worry, the Lord shall provide."

By then, Philander had escorted us to edge of his camp. Giving us a final shoo, he bustled back to his wagon. Without so much as a backwards look, he scurried inside, closing the flimsy wooden door behind him.

I waited until we were out of earshot, then whirled to face my so-called partner. "Have you gone plumb loco?" I screeched, waving my arms. "We couldn't afford to give away our money like that."

Bobby made a tisking sound and shook his head. "Now, Teddy, didn't you want to help those poor, unfortunate souls down in Utah?"

"Well, yeah," I stammered, shifting my feet. "Only, I ain't so sure—"

"You ain't so sure there ever was a flood?" Bobby finished for me. I nodded dumbly as Bobby chuckled. "Well, I'm sure there wasn't. You saw the way he turned down the blankets. Your good reverend was only interested in money. That whole cock-and-bull story was made up to shake some shekels outta our pockets."

"Yeah, and it worked," I grumbled sourly. "You gave him half our money."

"I didn't give it away, I invested it," Bobby assured, draping a heavy arm over my shoulders. "You see, Reverend Philander is going to provide us with our stake."

"Don't bet on it," I growled, shedding his arm from my shoulders. "I bet prying a nickel from his fingers would be harder than pulling a molar from a polar bear."

Bobby waved a hand and laughed. "You worry too much," he said. "When it comes to skinning a feller outta his money, a jasper like Philander is the easiest kind. Philander isn't even his name, you know."

"How do you know that?"

Bobby shrugged, rolling himself a smoke. "I was in Dodge when he brought his little act to town. He was calling himself Doctor Richard Philburn then. He was peddlin' some kind of cure-all."

"No, I meant how do you know he will be easy to skin? Seems like a mighty slick hombre to me."

"Yeah, but he's greedy. You take a feller

who's as greedy as the reverend, and he's always looking for a way to get rich. We're going to show him the way."

"What do you have in mind?" I asked, not at all sure I wanted to know.

"Well, by now, everyone knows Princess Catrinia is visiting the country. You can bet Philander has already been dreaming about laying his hands on her money and jewels. We'll simply tell him the truth, that we know the princess and are, in fact, helping her."

"What good will that do?" I demanded. "Do you even have a plan?"

"Well, no, not exactly, but that's the beauty of it," Bobby replied cheerfully. "We'll let Philander come up with the plan. You can bet the farm that once he hears of Catrinia, he'll come up with a way to separate her from her money."

Bobby grinned and rubbed his hands together, and I could tell he was downright pleased with himself. I was glad he was happy, 'cause I didn't have the foggiest idea how any of this was gonna help us. All I could think of was that it done cost us half our money.

As we neared the edge of town, I saw Bordeaux waiting. I wouldn't be able to duck him any longer. I didn't want to fight him, but that Frenchy wasn't giving me no choice. He called out to me as we started up the street.

"Any ideas?" I whispered to Bobby.

Bobby grinned and shrugged, seeming mighty unconcerned that I might have to kill a man or get killed myself. 'Course, I knew, it took a sight more than a gunbattle to ruffle Bobby Stamper's feathers. "Looks like you're gonna have to drill this feller," he said.

"Thanks for nothing," I said, growling and feeling a tightness in my stomach as we walked slowly up the street.

"Teddy, we got trouble," Bobby whispered as we closed the gap between us and the two Frenchmen.

As Bobby's words hit home, I felt a hot flash in my gut and a puckering in the seat of my drawers. "What is it?" I hissed.

"I caught a glimpse of a feller with a rifle on the roof of the hotel. He's ducked down behind the awning, and there's another man at the end of the street in the loft of the barn."

I couldn't see either man, and believe me, I looked real hard. I couldn't see them, but I believed they were there. Bobby never made mistakes like that. "Bordeaux must be serious," I said, battling to keep my tone casual.

"He means to salt your hide," Bobby agreed solemnly. "You gotta stall Bordeaux. I might be able to take the man on the hotel, but with a pistol, I wouldn't have a chance at hitting the man in the barn."

Bobby was right, somebody had set a trap and we'd blundered right into it. Once the shooting started, they meant to cut us to ribbons. And I didn't see any way to stop them.

Chapter Eight

Now, I never been a slick talking man, and Bordeaux didn't look to be in any mood to confab. His lips pale and clenched tight, he stared straight ahead as we approached.

His little buddy licked his lips and held out his hand. "My name is Robair Rosseau. I am Count Bordeaux's valet," he said, then went about explaining how this little shindig was gonna play out. They sure had a lot of rules about how a couple of fellers could settle their differences.

I could see that we were just about ready to fire off this little set-to, and I couldn't think of a way to stop it. I'd done tried saying I was sorry, but apologies ran off Bordeaux like water off a clay sidehill.

In the end, I did the only thing I could think of. I rared back and cut loose from the heels. That Frenchman saw the punch coming, but never had a chance to duck. Even as the look of surprise sprang to Bordeaux's face, my big fist splattered him right on the point of his chin. His feet shot right out from underneath him, and he lit flat on his back.

"Good job, Teddy!" Bobby said, whacking me on the back.

Even though Bobby whispered, that little Robair heard him. Anger replacing the shock on his face, he glared at us. "You would applaud such cowardly actions?" he demanded, almost screaming. "That was the most cowardly thing I have ever witnessed."

All of a sudden, now that I figured out I wasn't going on to the big reward in the sky, I begin to get sore. Fact is, I got downright mad. I jabbed a finger at the little man. "Oh, yeah," I roared. "Ain't no worse than him putting a man on the hotel roof and another in the barn, ready to shoot me down."

Well, by now, I was raving at the top of my lungs, and I got a full-grown set of them too. I don't reckon there was a soul in town who didn't hear me. Every man on the street followed my pointing finger up to the roof of the hotel. A gasp ran through the crowd, as we all saw a brief glimpse of a man and rifle, ducking down behind the false front.

"He's right!" a swarthy man in a checkered shirt shouted, shaking his fist. "Let's get the bushwhacking son of—" Whatever else he said was drowned out by a bloodthirsty roar as the crowd surged forward.

In less than two seconds, the street was completely empty, except for me and Bobby and the two Frenchmen. Robair Rosseau twisted his hands together, looking both confused and distressed. "You cannot possibly believe that the count had anything to do with this?" he wailed.

"Oh, yeah, anybody can see, the man's a saint," Bobby shot back.

In seconds, the crowd that rushed into the hotel was back, roughly dragging a man. "We caught the varmint!" the man in the checkered shirt said, shoving his captive out in the middle of the street.

A wild look in his eyes, the prisoner skidded to a halt just a few feet from me. I ran my eyes over him. He was tall and lean with greasy, stringy black hair and a jagged scar across his cheek. He was also no one I ever saw before.

As the men who had rushed to the barn came back, reporting that their man had escaped, the feller in the checkered shirt took charge. Brandishing the prisoner's rifle, he stepped right in front of the captive. "Why was you trying to kill that man?" he demanded, pointing back to me.

The condemned man licked his lips, glancing at the ring of unfriendly faces that pressed in at him. His face was white and his eyes wide and scared, but he refused to answer.

"Nothing to say, huh?" the man in the checkered shirt said, growling. He shook the rifle in the prisoner's face. "If you know what's good for you, you'll talk."

When the captured man still didn't answer, ol' checkered shirt whacked him in the chops with the butt of that rifle. He didn't really drive the butt of the rifle into the prisoner's face, it was more of a slap with the flat part of the stock. Still, it knocked the prisoner to his knees. On his hands and knees, the prisoner shook his head and spat blood into the dust of the street.

"Saul, what the devil is going on here?"

At the sound of the voice, we all turned to see a blocky man pushing through the crowd. He carried a shotgun in the crook of his arms, and a marshal's star hung from his shirt. Stopping in the middle of the street, he tugged at his drooping gray mustache, eyeing the crowd coolly. "I asked what all the excitement is about?"

Saul grounded the butt of his captured rifle and scratched his massive chest through that checkered shirt. "That varmint," he said, pointing an accusing finger down at the prisoner. "He tried to bushwhack that man," he explained as his finger swung to point at me.

The marshal studied me with a pair of cool brown eyes. "Is that right?" he asked and I nodded.

"I say we get a rope and string the polecat up," Saul said, and judging from the whooping and hollering from the crowd, they agreed.

That marshal, he never even turned a hair. He simply held up a hand and waited patiently for silence to reclaim the street. "There will be none of that here," he said quietly, but there was blue steel in his voice. I don't reckon too many men ever argued with this man. He fished a key from his vest pocket and held it out to a man in a fuzzy suit. "Henry, you and Jonsey take this man over to the jail and lock him up."

As the two men escorted the prisoner down the street, the marshal planted his worn boots right in front of me. "All right, suppose you tell me what started all of this?"

I shrugged uncomfortably, then glanced over at Bobby. "Well," I said, not knowing where to start. I pointed down at Bordeaux, who was still stretched out in the street. "Yesterday, me and that feller had a little up-scuddle over at the eatin' house."

"I heard about that," the marshal said crisply.

"Well, this morning, that Bardoo, he jumped us here on the street and said he wanted to settle things proper. I didn't want to kill him, but he weren't leaving me any choice. That's when my friend Bobby noticed that feller on the roof of the hotel and another jasper down in the barn loft."

The marshal held up his hand. "What happened to the man in the barn?"

"Sorry, Tom. He got away," Saul said.

"Okay," Marshal Tom grunted, pulling at his mustache. "Then what happened?"

I rammed my hands down in my pockets and shifted my feet. "Well, I knew if any shooting started, them fellers was gonna open up. I couldn't think of anything else to do, so I hauled off and swatted Bordeaux."

The marshal nodded once, then ran his

eyes over the crowd. "That pretty much the way it happened?"

A chorus of "yes sirs" and "looked that-aways" came from the crowd. That seemed to satisfy the marshal, cause he nodded grimly. He pointed the shotgun one-handed down at Robair and Bordeaux, who, under Robair's flitting care, had managed to set up. "You two, come with me."

Now that wallop upside the jaw took some of the starch outta Bordeaux's drawers, but not all of it, and it never even put a dent in his highfalutin manner. Slapping away Robair's attempts to help, he climbed to his feet. Standing very straight, he pulled down his short jacket with an angry jerk. "I will not," he stated flatly.

The marshal smiled tiredly and tapped Bordeaux in the chest with the muzzle of that shotgun. "Oh, yes, you will. You're under arrest."

"Arrest!" Robair Rosseau squealed, his hand flying to his face. "That is Count Paul Bordeaux! You cannot arrest him!"

The smile remained on the marshal's face, and I swear, I thought I saw a twinkle in his faded brown eyes. "I don't care if he's the Queen of England. I'm running this town." The marshal's voice had been friendly, but now a hint of snow crept into his tone. "Now march."

As the pair stumbled off in the direction of the jail, the marshal turned to me and Bobby. "Stamper, I want you and your friend to tag along. I still got a couple of things I want to clear up." The marshal grinned at the shocked looks that I knew were galloping across our faces. "Bobby Stamper. Oh, yeah, I recognized you."

As we tagged along, I could hear the excited whispers whipping through the crowd. I reckon everybody in the world had heard of Bobby Stamper, and evidently so had these folks. I leaned in close to Bobby and whispered in his ear. "I hope to heaven you never robbed the bank in this town."

I think, for the first time ever, I saw an expression of concern riding on Bobby's face. "You know, I just can't remember."

"That's just great!" I hissed. "We're liable to find ourselves in jail."

Right then, when Bobby didn't have a wisecrack, I knew we were in deep trouble. "I've seen that marshal before," was all he said.

Halfway to the jail, we met up with the marshal's helpers. The man in the fuzzy suit held out the key. "There you go, Tom. He's locked up safe and sound. You need anything else?"

"No, Henry, thanks," the marshal said, taking the key and giving the two Frenchmen a shove. "Get along, we're almost there."

When we reached the jail, the marshal stepped back, waving us all inside. "Have a seat," he offered, waving to a bunch of straight-backed chairs that littered the office. As we slid into the chairs, the marshal hung his shotgun on a rack, then crossed to a heavy, wooden door in the back wall. A heavy piece of canvas hung from the door, and as the marshal picked up one corner of the canvas, I could see a small hole about a foot square in the door. I figured the door must lead back to the cells, 'cause the marshal looked for a second, then said, "You just set tight, we'll get to you in good time."

That done, he dropped the canvas and took a seat behind the desk. Seated comfortably, he rolled a smoke, his eyes measuring each of us. "All right," he said, whipping a match across the top of his desk. "Tell me all about it," he said around the cigarette.

As the marshal brought the match up to his cigarette, Bordeaux shot to his feet. "This man insulted me and attacked me physically!"

"Yeah, I heard all about it," the marshal said, staring at me through a cloud of smoke. "You're a big man," he observed dryly. "You get your jollies out of smacking around fellers half your size?"

"No," I answered. "But he left me little choice."

"So you say," the marshal replied calmly. He took a last, long puff of his smoke, then stabbed it out on the scarred desktop. "What I want to know about is the feller I got in my jail." His voice cold as well water, the marshal flicked the dead cigarette into the corner and looked square at Bordeaux. "I'm wondering if you didn't hire him for a little insurance. Just to make sure you hadn't bit off more than you could chew."

Boiling blood raced up Bordeaux's neck, coloring his face dark red. I reckon, if he woulda had a gun, he woulda shot the marshal dead right then and there. Since he didn't have a shooter handy, he settled for pointing a trembling finger. "How dare you, sir! I am count Paul Bordeaux! I need no help to deal with a common thug such as him."

The marshal's expression didn't even flicker as he rose to his feet. "Look, Count, you may cut the fat hogs where you come from, but that don't mean doodly squat here," the marshal said evenly. When he decided to make his move, the marshal jumped so quick, it startled us all. Like a striking snake, the marshal grabbed the front of Bordeaux's coat and dragged the Frenchman halfway across the desk. "This is my town," the marshal said, his faces inches from Bordeaux's. "You want to show what a big man you are by killing some poor slob, do it somewhere else. You start any more trouble here, and I'll fan your backside and send you packing. Now get outta my sight!" His speech finished, the marshal released Bordeaux with a shove.

For a second, Bordeaux reminded me of a stallion in a pen full of mares. His face red as a strawberry patch and his nostrils flaring, the Frenchman pawed the floor. For a wild second, I sure figured he would tie into the sheriff. He never done it. Spinning around like a parade soldier, he shoved Robair out of the way. His back ramrod straight, Bordeaux stormed to the door, his heels clicking with each step.

The marshal waited until he was at the door, then spoke quietly. "Bordeaux, if I find out you had anything to do with hiring that man in my cell, I'll squash you like a stink-bug."

Bordeaux's body seemed to curl up like a

piece of green leather left in the sun, but he never said a word as he threw open the door and stalked outside.

Wringing his hands and fritting around like a drunken sparrow, Robair looked out the open door, then back at the marshal. "If you gentlemen will excuse me," he said hesitantly.

"Get," the marshal said with a wave of his hand. "And close the door behind you."

As the door closed, the marshal tore open a desk door and came out with a bottle and glass. "Now, for you two," he muttered, yanking the cork from the bottle. He poured the glass full, replaced the stopper in the bottle and dropped it back in the drawer without even bothering to offer us a snort. He raised the glass, pausing to study us over the rim. "What brings you two to my town?"

"Just passing through," Bobby replied as the marshal downed his drink.

A snorting laugh escaped past the marshal's lips as he slammed the glass down on the desk. "If I recall right, that's exactly what you said in Tombstone."

"They never proved anything," Bobby shot back cheerfully. "I got it now!" he exclaimed, his face lighting up like someone shoved a candle in his ear. "You're Tom Herndon!"

"That's right," the marshal said crisply. "I was working for Wells Fargo then. I spent three months trying to pin that job on you."

Bobby smiled and slapped his knee. "Well, I know you're a good man. If you couldn't nail me, then it must mean that I never done it."

"Yeah, right," Herndon snorted sarcastically. He arched his eyebrows at us. "You two wouldn't be thinking that with all these folks in town, this would be a fine time to hit our bank?"

"No, sir," I said quickly. "My name is Teddy Cooper. Now, if you—"

"I done figured out who you are," Marshal Herndon interrupted.

"Good," I said, hitching up straighter in my chair. "Then you must know that I'm a fellow lawman?"

Something in what I said musta tickled Herndon's funnybone, 'cause he slapped his desk and hooted loudly. "Lawman? You actually call yourself a lawman? Like I said, I been hearing stories about you. You ain't exactly running a boys' school over there in Whiskey City."

I felt my face color as I tried to shrug off his remarks. I reckon, I knew as a lawman I wouldn't make a patch on his backside, but it didn't seem neighborly for him to point it out. "We had some troubles," I admitted, and it sounded lame even to me. "But we handled them."

Herndon frowned, tugging at his mustache again. "Yeah, I heard you took out Butch Adkins and Dave Hetfield. Them was some raunchy boys. I guess you done us all a favor."

"We did what we had to do."

"Yeah," the marshal agreed dryly. He pulled the bottle back out of his desk. "You might be a lawman after all, but you're running in bad company."

Bobby grinned innocently and spread his hands in front of him. "Hey, Marshal, I'm a ree-formed man. I'm married and everything."

"Yeah, I heard that too," Herndon said as he poured his glass back full. He pounded the cork back into the bottle, then his eyes met Bobby's. "Can't say as I believe it, even yet."

His face solemn as a judge's, Bobby raised his right hand. "It's the gospel."

Herndon grunted out a couple of cuss words, then reached inside his desk, yanking out two more glasses. "Okay, I'll take your word for it," he said, tossing us each a glass. "Now, suppose you cut out all the nonsense and tell me; why are you really here?"

"It's a long story," I said, snaggin' the bottle out of the air with one hand.

Herndon took a sip, then leaned back, propping his feet up on the desk. "Suppose you tell it to me."

"Well, I reckon you heard tell about Princess Catrinia from Russia making a tour through the country?" I asked as I poured my glass brim full. Herndon nodded as I passed the bottle to Bobby. "She got herself into a spot of trouble. We helped her out, but we found out there's some men gonna try and snuff her dad, the king."

"Czar," Herndon corrected, sipping his whiskey. "In Russia, they call their kings czars."

"Yeah, well, whatever you want to call him, somebody wants to make him dead."

"Who?" Herndon asked, sweeping his feet off the desk and sitting up straight.

"Some of his own men," Bobby answered. "They tried to kidnap the princess. When that blew up on them they robbed our bank. We been trailing them all the way from Whiskey City."

Herndon took a sip, then studied the whiskey in his glass. "You think they hired that man? Trying to slow you down a little?"

I looked at Bobby and we both shrugged.

Herndon finished the drink and tossed the glass into the drawer. "What do you say we go ask him?" he suggested.

As Marshal Herndon unlocked the heavy door that led back to the cells, Bobby and I finished our drinks. Herndon swung the door wide and we all stepped inside. We barely set foot in the back room before we all stopped dead in our tracks.

One the other side of a narrow walkway were three cells. In the corner cell, the prisoner lay slumped in a pool of his own blood. His mouth twisted, he stared up at us with eyes that would never see again. Shining brightly through the barred window, the rays of the morning sun glistened off the silver knife sticking from the man's throat.

Chapter Nine

There wasn't a thing we could do for the man in the cell. He was dead as a man can get. With Herndon leading the way and me and Bobby follering, we turned and pounded out the door. We all stopped on the boardwalk, our eyes roaming the street, searching for any suspicious-looking characters. It weren't no use.

The street was crammed with people coming and going as they waited for the trials to resume in the afternoon. There musta been fifty people in sight and any one of them could've been the killer.

Herndon was a man who knew his business. He didn't waste any time on staring at the crowded street. "Let's circle around back.

You two go that way," he barked, pulling his pistol. "I'll circle around the other way. Keep your eyes open for tracks."

As Herndon went around the east side of the building, Bobby and I took the west. We didn't see anyone, nor any fresh tracks. When we completed our circle, we found Herndon squatting under the window on the east side. "Find anything?" I asked.

"Not much," Herndon replied, wiping his palms on his jeans as he straightened up. He gestured to some drag marks on the ground. "The killer dragged a blanket or something behind him to wipe out his tracks."

"Smart cuss," I commented sourly. "Whoever the killer is, he must have known we would get around to questioning that man and decided to finish him off 'fore we got the chance."

"The killer took a big chance," Herndon decided, rubbing the stubble on his chin. "He had no way of knowing we'd stall around like we did. For all he knew, we'd already be back in the cell, raking that feller over the coals."

"Maybe he did know," Bobby said slowly. "If Bordeaux was the killer, he knew when he left the jail, you was planning on talking with us for a while. All he had to do was circle around the jail and run that sticker into that feller's neck."

Herndon's eyebrows went up as he nodded absently. "That was a fancy blade," he admitted. "Looked like something that fancy dude might carry."

"That don't hardly make sense," I protested. "I mean, sure me and him had a little difference of opinion, but he wouldn't hire someone to kill me. That man wanted to do the job himself."

"Maybe," Bobby said, rubbing the side of his face. "Or just maybe that was all an act. We know Fedarov hired an assassin. How do we know that Bordeaux wasn't that man?"

"He sure looks like a man that could look you straight in the eye and shoot you dead," Herndon agreed. He scowled and pulled at his mustache a couple of times. "I think we best go have a chat with him."

With that decided, we walked down the alley toward the hotel. As we walked, we could see the drag marks in the dust where the killer had dragged something behind him to wipe out his tracks. We shared a quick glance between us. The killer had definitely came out of the back of the hotel.

Without a word, we walked grimly around the hotel to the front. Just as we rounded the hotel, we bumped into Robair Rosseau. The little dude had his sleeves rolled up and carried a silver tray.

"Where's your boss?" Herndon growled.

"In his hotel room," Rosseau answered, a slight tremor in his voice. "After this morning's encounter, the count said he wasn't feeling well and wanted to lie down and rest. He sent me down to the store for some soda for his stomach and a powder for his head."

"That's a handy excuse," Bobby said dryly as we exchanged a glance. "While Junior here was down at the store, it woulda been real easy for Bordeaux to slip down the alley to the jail," he suggested, leaving the rest unsaid.

"Whatever are you talking about?" Robair asked.

"Somebody slipped down the alley, reached in the window, and slid a knife into the throat of my prisoner," Herndon said harshly. He pulled himself up to his full height and glared down at the little Frenchman. "You wouldn't know anything about that?"

Right then, I kinda felt sorry for the little man. His hands holding the tray trembled slightly, and he looked like he was gonna have himself an accident. "Dear me, that is simply horrible," he said. Then the realization downed on his face. "And you think the count is responsible?" he said accusingly.

"That's exactly what we think," Herndon said, growling. "We'd like to have a word with him. What room is he in?"

"His is the back corner room on the second floor," Robair answered. "But I assure you, the count would have nothing to do with such a dastardly act of cowardice."

"We'll see about that," Herndon said. "Now, take us up to his room."

Rosseau led the way as we tromped through the lobby and up the stairs. When we reached Bordeaux's door, Herndon shoved Robair out of the way and pounded heavily on the door. Herndon shifted his feet impatiently and raised his hand to knock again, when Bordeaux swung the door open.

I looked him over close; if had just slipped out of the building and down the alley and knifed a man to death, Bordeaux hid it well. He had no blood on his hands, and his expression was bleary, but the tone in his voice was cold. "What do you want now?" he asked.

"Somebody just killed that man in my jail," Herndon said bluntly. "You know anything about that?"

Cold fury swept across Bordeaux's clean-shaven face. I don't reckon he woulda been any madder if Herndon had slapped him. "Of course not!"

"Okay," Herndon replied. "Sorry to have bothered you."

Herndon backed away from the door, pushing me and Bobby back down the hall. I waited until we were down the hall a ways, and Robair was in Bordeaux's room, then whirled to face the marshal. "Is that all you are going to do?" I demanded.

"For the moment," Herndon replied calmly.

"What?" Bobby exclaimed. "I say we go back there and get the truth out of him. He killed that feller, I'd bet my bottom dollar on it."

"Likely," Herndon replied, stopping and facing us. "Do you really think he would tell us anything?"

"Probably not," I admitted, my voice surly. "But it wouldn't hurt to ask him a few questions."

"It wouldn't help any either," Herndon replied. "Man like Bordeaux wouldn't tell you anything. All it would do is waste a lot of time. I want to get started asking around town. There's so many folks in town, I'm willing to bet that somebody saw something."

Herndon started down the stairs, then stopped halfway down. "You boys said you were rushing to California to save that Russian king. Well, I suggest that you don't dally around and get on about it."

I started to point out that we were a mite short of horses and money, but Marshal Herndon never gave me a chance. Without another word, he turned and clopped down the stairs.

I turned to Bobby, who was leaning against the wall, rolling himself a smoke. "I think we best round us up some money and get out of here," I decided.

"Yeah," Bobby agreed. "I was thinking the same thing."

As Bobby lit his cigarette, a door opened down the hall and Lilly Simmons breezed into the hallway. Twirling her fancy umbrella, she smiled at us. "Teddy, Bobby, how nice to see you again," she said brightly.

"Good to see you too, Miss Lilly," I said, sweeping my hat off as Bobby sucked on his cigarette and grunted a greeting.

"I was just preparing to go down for lunch. Perhaps you would like to join me? I would be happy to pay."

I tell you at the very mention of lunch, my stomach jumped up and waved a flag. I was so hungry, I could eat a buzzard, feathers and all. "Why, ma'am, that's right kind of you. I'd be happy to join you."

"Good," Lilly said, then turned to Bobby. "Will you be joining us?"

"I think I'll pass," he replied coolly. Without another word, he pushed away from the wall and tromped down the stairs.

Lilly frowned at his retreating back. "I'm afraid that Bobby still hasn't forgiven me yet. Not that I can blame him," Lilly said softly. "I've done some terrible things."

"Aw, don't worry about him. He'll come around. He's just stubborn, that's all," I said, wanting to get the subject off Bobby and back on eating.

Lilly smiled beautifully and took my arm. "Let's go eat."

Bobby stepped out of the hotel, stopping on the boardwalk to survey the street. He swore and spat into the dust. Teddy was a nice guy, tough as a boot when he had to be, but he was way too trusting. A good man himself, Teddy always looked for the good in people.

Bobby knew different. He'd been around and seen enough people to know that most folks had plenty of the old nick in them. Bobby wasn't buying Lilly's newfound righteousness. A woman like Lilly didn't change. She was probably still trying to cheat Teddy out of his silver mine.

Silver mine! Bobby swore quickly. Then a slow smile spread across his face as an idea grew in his brain. Bobby Stamper was a quick man who moved with a lively step, but now he was almost running as he hurried down the street.

When he reached Philander's revival tent, Bobby paused to catch his breath and plan what he was going to say. Taking a deep breath, he pulled back the flap and stepped inside.

Reverend Philander stood at the pulpit, practicing a sermon. Predictably, he was extolling the virtues of charity, quoting Scripture when it suited his purpose.

"Very good," Bobby said, clapping his hands. "You've come a long ways, Doctor Philburn."

At the mention of his old name, Philander let his hands fall to his side, a wary look on his face as he stepped away from the pulpit. "Bobby Stamper," he said accusingly, "I should have recognized you this morning. Who was that big deadwood you was dragging around?"

"His name is Teddy Cooper," Bobby said,

taking a seat on the bench that served as a pew. "In fact, he's part of the reason I came to see you. I'm going to need your help."

"Maybe I don't want to help you."

The smile on Bobby's face widened as he propped his feet up on the bench in front of him. "Oh, I think you will want to help me," Bobby said, leaning back and clasping his hands behind his head. "Unless you want me to go have a chat with the marshal. Clue him in to your background. I bet he'd be right interested to hear about some of the shenanigans you've pulled."

The reverend had been more or less expecting this, but still had trouble keeping the panic off his face and out of his voice. He shrugged, trying to appear unconcerned. "I was a different person then. Ruled by greed and pleasures of the flesh. Today, I stand before you a changed man."

"Yeah, I bet," Bobby said and grunted. He was struck by the fact that this was the second person in as many days who tried to tell him they'd turned over a new leaf. Bobby no more believed Philander than he had Lilly.

"I no longer lust after money and the company of scandalous women," Philander said. "I find peace in carrying out God's plan."

"The only way you're working on God's

plan is if He wants these folks separated from their money."

"Charity is a part of His work," Philander said sullenly.

Bobby laughed, slapping a knee. "The way you do it, I'm sure it is," he jeered. "Now, are you going to help me, or do I have to go have a chat with the marshal? Tom Herndon is a savvy man, and a mighty impatient one. He won't stand for you stealing from his people."

The sagging of Philander's shoulders signaled his defeat. "What do you want?" he asked.

Right then, Bobby had a decision to make. He could simply ask for the money they needed. Quickly he figured in his head the price of four horses, saddles, and gear—plus supplies, and they would need a little folding money to see them through. It came to a good sum, likely close to what Philander would pull out of this town. Bobby had a sneaky feeling that if he asked for that much, Philander would call his bluff. It would be cheaper for the reverend to simply pull stakes and move to the next town.

With a sigh, Bobby knew, he'd have to do this the hard way. "Actually, Reverend, this is right up your alley. In fact, if you help me, you could stand to rake in a good pile."

The mention of money grabbed Philander's attention by the short hairs. He was wary, but he was also greedy. "What do you have in mind?" he asked, taking a small step forward.

"That feller Teddy Cooper, he's a sap. I've been playing him for a couple of weeks now."

Philander frowned, a hard look of suspicion galloping across his face. "I never knew you to run a con."

Bobby shrugged. "Robbing banks was getting too hot. Too many folks knew about me, so I figured it was time for a change. I used to hang around Little Jimmy Shaw when I was a kid. I picked up a few things."

"Jimmy Shaw," Philander whispered, with more reverence in his voice for the old conman than he had when he was preaching. "Jimmy was the best," Philander acknowledged, pulling a bench close to Bobby and setting down. "What's the deal? That hillbilly don't look like he has a dime to his name." Philander stopped suddenly, the hard look of suspicion blowing back across his face. "He don't! I saw him this morning. He had trouble raking two cents together!"

"That's right," Bobby said, grinning wickedly. "But the fool has a silver mine. It's worth millions."

"Silver mine!" Philander croaked. Greed and distrust fought for control of his face, and greed won hands down. Hitching his bench an inch closer, he leaned close to Bobby. "Tell me about it."

Bobby smiled; he had Philander hooked now. "The boob doesn't know about the silver. He thinks it's just a played-out gold mine."

"So all we have to do is get him to sell it to us."

Bobby shook his head, cutting Philander's enthusiasm off at the pass. "He won't sell. Dang hick says there's no gold in the mine, and he don't want to cheat nobody by selling it to them."

Philander was almost frothing at the mouth. "A man that dumb and that honest, well, that's a gift. We can't let him get away," Philander said, rubbing his hands together.

"I've tried every game I can remember, but he ain't took the bait yet." Wanting to laugh out loud, Bobby plastered a rueful look on his face. "I even staged that holdup, thinking that if he was broke, he might sell."

"Sounds good. Is he ready to deal?"

"Maybe," Bobby admitted, rubbing his chin. "But like you said, this ain't my bag of tricks and I made a big mistake."

"What kind of mistake?"

"Well, to make it look good, I had to get robbed myself. Now, I'm supposed to be broke. If I suddenly come up with the money to buy him out . . . Well, even a boob like Cooper might get wise."

"That's where I come in," Philander offered, catching on quickly.

"That's right, but we gotta move fast. We got competition."

"Competition?" Philander muttered, a frown washing the greedy smile from his lips. "Who? Can we have them killed?"

"No," Bobby replied with a slow shake of his head. "It's a woman, her name is Lilly Simmons. She's over at the hotel, working on him right now."

"Lilly!" Philander exploded, shooting to his feet. "That two-timing little wench."

"You know her?" Bobby asked, both surprised and concerned.

"She works for me!" Philander raged, stalking back and forth up the aisle between the pews.

"Works for you?" Bobby asked, his mind racing as he tried to decide how this affected his plans.

"Yeah, I use her to rope in business. She walks around town, talking to the men. When they hear that she is going to sing, they pack the place. Then if collections are slow, I have her come up and tell of the suffering we see. After she sheds a few tears, the collection plates really start to fill up." Philander stopped his pacing, smacking his fist into his palm. "I taught her this game from top to bottom, and now you tell me she's double-crossing me? Working a sap behind my back? Just wait until I get my hands on her."

"That might not be wise," Bobby cautioned, then nodded his head emphatically. "Yes, that is the last thing we want to do. Cooper trusts me. He won't do anything without talking to me first. We don't want to tip Lilly off that there's another pig at the trough."

Slowly cooling down, Philander nodded grimly. "That is wise," he said, then resumed his pacing. "How are you going to play it?"

"I'm still not sure," Bobby said, showing his teeth in a daring smile. "I'm playing it by ear, but I could sure use some folding money."

That almost erased the smile from Philander's face, but he was hooked now. He grudgingly passed a few dollars to Bobby. "You double-cross me, Stamper, and you'll never be able to run far enough," he snarled.

Bobby laughed, carelessly ramming the money down in his pocket. "You just have the money ready. I imagine it'll take four hundred at least to buy him out."

"Four hundred! That's a lot," Philander said, worried. "How do we know the mine is worth that much?"

"You could telegraph the assayer's office in Kansas City. They tested the ore samples."

"There's no telegraph in Beaver Falls," Philander said, a touch of anger in his voice.

"Is that a fact?" Bobby asked innocently. "Well, I guess you'll just have to trust me."

Bobby left the tent, his mind busy, wondering if he had looked before he leaped. Now that the fish had taken the bait, how to set the hook? Bobby knew Teddy didn't want to sell his mine, not for no four hundred dollars. How to get the money from Philander without signing over the mine?

As he walked back into town, Bobby tried to recall all the games Jimmy had run. Jimmy had been the master, knowing a thousand ways for every situation to take a man's money. Mines had been a large part of Jimmy's arsenal, but Bobby couldn't remember how Jimmy did it. At the time, Bobby had been more concerned with learning how to crack safes.

As he turned up the street, Bobby saw Lester and Elmo coming toward him. For a fleet-

ing second, Bobby considered ducking
between two buildings, but it was already too
late. The brothers had already spotted him.
As they drew closer, Bobby could see from
their expressions that they weren't nowhere
near happy.

Their long faces bright red, they stopped
square in the middle of the street, hooking
their thumbs in their gun belts as they
waited. "Where the devil is everybody?" Elmo
squawked.

"Yeah, we woke up this morning and everybody was gone," Lester bawled. "We was beginning to think you fellers was trying to give
us the slip."

Now, there's an idea, Bobby thought. For a
second, he savored the thought of losing the
two brothers, but then, he knew it would
never work. Lester and Elmo were like un-
wanted stray dogs—every time you tried to
get rid of them, they beat you home.

So Bobby smiled and stepped between the
brothers, placing his arms over their shoulders. "Naw, we wouldn't do that," he assured,
flashing them a big grin. "It was just that you
fellers was sleeping so hard, we figured you
needed the rest."

"I was a mite pooped," Lester admitted.

"Bet you're hungry too. I rounded us up

some spending money. Let's find the others and get something to eat."

Like a glob of spit on a hot rock, Lester and Elmo's bad humor disappeared. Once again, as they jumped up and down, begging to eat, they reminded Bobby of two stray dogs. If they had tails, Bobby knew they'd be wagging right now. Bobby shook his head. He figured somebody had to take care of these two, might as well be him.

Lester smacked his lips and rubbed his belly. "Boy, I'm more than ready to eat. I could eat the hide off a horse."

"I don't doubt it," Bobby laughed. "Let's find the others."

"Teddy's in the eatin' house right now," Elmo growled. "He's with that fancy woman."

A worried look jumped up and landed on Elmo's face with both feet. "I don't like her," he announced. "She scares the fire outta me."

"Yeah, she bothers me some too," Bobby agreed. "Where's Joe?"

Lester and Elmo exchanged blank looks, then shrugged. "How should we know? We ain't seen him all day," Elmo said.

"Well, let's round him up. I'm starved," Bobby said.

Bobby figured, knowing Joe, he would be in the saloon, but a check of the place didn't turn him up. From the saloon, they went through the whole town, looking high and low, but they never found Joe. It was as if he disappeared from the face of the earth.

After her lunch with Teddy, Lilly returned to her hotel room. She wanted to get out of the heat and rest before she had to sing at the meeting tonight. When she opened her door, she saw a man seated on her bed. "Sergei, what are you doing here? What if someone saw you come in here?" she said worriedly, sticking her head into the hall and looking both ways before closing the door.

A smile played on Sergei Bronski's lips, but it did not extend to his eyes. "Have no fear. No one saw me," he said, his accented voice soft. "I see that you act quickly. I hear that one of the conspirators has been eliminated. This is good. Time is of the essence. The others must be dealt with quickly."

"But, Sergei—" Lilly started to protest, but Bronski place two fingers on her lips, silencing her.

"We must have no doubts now. Everything is ready now. The future of my country is at stake. They must be neutralized."

A sick feeling in her stomach, Lilly glanced at the worn boards on the floor. She knew that by "neutralized" Sergei meant he wanted them dead.

Chapter Ten

Iwas full as a stuffed pillow when I plopped down on the bench out in front of the hotel. As I lazed in the shade, a good feeling washed over me. It done my heart good to see someone like Lilly make changes in her life.

A warm feeling in my belly, I leaned back and closed my eyes. I didn't get long to enjoy the peaceful feeling. Seemed like I just got my eyes screwed shut when Bobby, Lester, and Elmo pounded up. They all tried to talk at once, and I couldn't make heads or tails about what they were saying. My neck was getting sore from swinging from one to the other when Bobby finally silenced them with a savage sweep of his arm. "Teddy, have you seen Joe?" he asked.

"No," I said, stretching my arms and fighting off a yawn. "Not since I left camp this morning. What's the problem?"

"Problem is, we cain't find him," Elmo sputtered.

I frowned, looking up at Bobby, who nodded grimly. "We went through this town from top to bottom. He ain't here," Bobby said.

I was concerned, but not really worried. I mean, Joe ain't the most sociable feller. "Likely went off on his own. You know how he is," I said, trying to shrug it off. "He'll be around sooner or later."

"Maybe," Bobby allowed but he couldn't dismiss it so easy. "Somebody sure tried to keep us from making it to California," he said, taking a seat on the bench beside me. "I mean, they already took a stab at sending me and you to Boot Hill. Suppose they tried the same thing with Joe?"

Well now, he had a point. Whoever was trying to stop us wasn't playing tiddlywinks. They had killed their own man to keep him from talking. They wouldn't hesitate a second to kill one of us. I stood up slowly. "You think we should go talk with the marshal?"

"Might not hurt," Bobby decided. "I'd rather cry wolf than let something happen to Joe."

"What about eating? I thought we was gonna go get us some grub," Lester said in a whiny voice and pouting.

Bobby dug down in his pocket, and danged if he didn't come out with some money. "You guys go ahead. Me and Teddy will catch up with you later," he said, handing half of the cash to them.

Like two kids fighting over a piece of rock candy, Lester and Elmo started up the street, scraping over the money. I watched them a second, then turned to Bobby and raised my eyebrows. "Looks like you been busy," I commented as he stuffed what was left of his wad back into his jeans. "Where'd you get the money?" I asked, almost cringing from the answer.

"The Reverend Philander gave it to me," Bobby said with a wide grin.

"Philander? I can't hardly believe that. Why in the world would that old skinflint give you any money?"

Bobby whacked me across the back, grinning broadly. "Because I told him about your silver mine."

I groaned and shook my head. "I wish you hadn't done that," I said. That danged mine had already caused me too much grief. Sometimes I almost wished I had never even heard of it.

"Don't worry. I can handle Philander," Bobby said cheerfully. "I told him I was going to skin you out of that mine and that I might need his help to turn the trick."

"What'd he say to that?"

Bobby chuckled. "He jumped at it so fast, he like to come out of his boots. He didn't even bat an eye when I asked him for some walking-around money. Why, I bet he's over there right now, counting the money he thinks he'll make off your mine."

"Probably," I admitted, Philander struck me as a greedy cuss. I stopped dead in the middle of the street, scratching my head. "I don't see how that is gonna make us any money, though," I confessed.

When that devil-may-care smile sprang to Bobby's face, I groaned again. We were in for it. Bobby didn't have all the answers. As if to prove me right, Bobby laughed and said, "Now, I ain't rightly got the plan all worked out, but don't you fret, it'll come to me in good time."

"Humph," I grunted, casting my eyes up at the sky.

We walked down the street a ways in silence, and when Bobby spoke, he was dead serious. "Teddy, if I was you, I'd stay away from Lilly," he said, grabbing my arm and pulling me to a stop. "I'd bet a dollar agin a cowpie that she's still scheming of a way to separate you from that mine."

"No," I explained patiently. "She told me she's changed and I believe her."

Bobby snorted and spat on the ground. "Teddy, she's working for Philander, helping him rope folks in so he can take their money."

"I know, she told me," I informed him. "In fact, that's what changed her. Now, she knows Philander is phony as a two-dollar bill, but just being around all of the preaching got her to thinking. She took to reading the Good Book and 'fore she knew it, she went and caught herself a dose of religion."

"She told you that?"

"She shore did."

"Teddy, I swear, it's a lucky thing for you that I'm here to look after you. Didn't it ever even occur to you that she might just be making all that up?" Bobby snorted again and shook his head. "Her getting religion? Fat chance. Why, even if she won a bet with Saint Peter, that woman couldn't get into heaven."

Now, I never saw it thataway, but I saw no sense in jawing all day about it. Bobby done made up his mind, and I knew it was easier to change the color of the sky than change his mind. Besides, by then, we were at the jail.

We pushed through the door and found Marshal Herndon staring at a collection of junk piled on his desk. He glanced up at us and his expression turned to sour milk.

Trying to be polite, I smiled. "You find out anything?" I asked.

"Not much. So far, nobody I've talked to saw anyone lurking around in the alley behind the jail." Herndon sighed and leaned back in his chair. "I'll keep trying, there's so many people on the street, somebody had to notice something," he said, then waved to the pile on his desk. "I was just going through the dead man's things. I found out his name was Nelson Buckly. That mean anything to either of you?"

I shook my head; I had never heard that name before. "Doesn't ring any bells, Tom," Bobby replied.

"Well, I've heard of him," Herndon said, surprising us both. Herndon picked up a coin from the pile and twirled it through his fingers. "When I was down in Arizona. He was hanging around, selling scalps and generally getting into trouble. A man was robbed and killed and there was talk of a hanging, but

Buckly drifted out of the country before one could be organized." Herndon sighed and tossed the coin back onto the pile. "I reckon whoever killed him done the world a favor."

"Likely you're right," I agreed. In my book, a scalp hunter was a notch or two lower than a snake. I wasn't gonna shed no tears for him. I shook my head, getting back down to business. "That wasn't the only reason we came over here. One of our friends is missing."

"Missing? What do you mean missing?"

"I mean nobody's seen him since this morning. We looked all through the town. He ain't here," I answered.

Herndon grimaced and tugged at his mustache. "That don't mean nothing," he decided. "There's so many folks coming and going around town, it'd be easy to miss him."

Bobby was already shaking his head. "No, Tom. We turned this town inside out looking for him. He ain't here."

Marshal Herndon leaned forward, resting his elbows on the desk. "Look, boys, your friend is a grown man. I'm sure he can take care of himself. He probably found himself a girl or went out for a ride."

"Then you won't help us find him?"

"No, Bobby, I haven't got the time," Herndon said, raking Buckly's meager pile of belongings off into a desk drawer. "If he don't show by morning, then I'll get excited."

"That may be too late," I protested.

Herndon grinned wryly and shook his head. "I doubt that. You wait; he'll turn up."

We didn't like it much, but there wasn't a lot we could do about it. Bidding the marshal good day, we tromped back out into the street. Once outside, Bobby grabbed my arm. "Teddy, I'm getting a bad feeling about this place."

"What do you mean?" I asked, but I kinda felt the same uneasy feeling crawling up the back of my spine.

"I mean there's somebody out to get us, and we don't know who. Fedarov coulda hired anybody. There's too many people in this town, and any man we see might be the one waiting for his chance to kill us."

"What are you saying?" I asked, taking my hat off and running my fingers through my sweat-dampened hair.

"I'm saying I would feel better out on the trail where we can see them coming. I'm saying we should go see Philander and squeeze money out of him, find Joe, and then get the heck outta here."

I looked down in the crown of my hat, wiping the sweat from the band with my finger.

Bobby's warnings worried me more than my own uneasy instincts. Bobby Stamper wasn't a man who spooked easy. He'd just grin at things that would rattle the knees of most men. If Bobby was running scared, it might be time to hit the trail.

"You might be right," I said, slapping the hat back on my head. "Besides, if we want to catch Fedarov, we best be shaking a leg."

"Good," Bobby replied with a smile. "Let's go see Philander."

We would have never found it, if we weren't a bit lazy. Instead of walking down to the end of the street, and then taking the trail out to Philander's tent, we went between the buildings and cut cross country.

Clumping along in the knee-high grass, we literally tripped over the body. As I looked down to see what my big toe hooked over, I saw the hand thrown wide. The breath caught in my throat as my eyes traveled up his body to his chalk white face. "Is he dead?" Bobby asked as I fell to my knees.

A lump stuck in my throat and my eyes burning, I touched the cold flesh of Joe Haven's face. "Yeah, he's dead."

Jack Warren didn't like taking orders and he didn't like being summoned like he was a schoolboy being called up before the head-master. Despite his anger, Jack Warren was cautious. He made sure no one saw him as he circled around to the rear of the livery stable.

Behind the stable was a corral, filled with several horses, then farther back a large stack of loose grass hay. It was behind the haystack that Jack found the man he sought. "All right, Mikhail, what do you want?"

"I want you to do the job you were paid for," Mikhail replied coldly.

"We're trying," Warren said. "It isn't easy with so many people in town. It might be easier to wait until they are out on the trail."

"No! There is too much chance of losing them. I want it done today!"

"Okay, we'll try," Jack agreed. "But the marshal has one of my men in jail. We need to do something about that."

Mikhail smiled. "Do not worry about him. I have already taken care of him."

It took a second to dawn on Jack what those words meant. When it did, a slow flush crept up his neck. "You killed him!" he accused angrily.

Mikhail shrugged casually. "I did what was necessary."

"I oughta kill you for that," Warren threatened.

"You won't," Mikhail said calmly. "Now, you have been paid to do a job; go do it."

Warren's hand was on his gun, and he almost used it. Slowly he relaxed. What did Nelson Buckly mean to him? Nothing. He was just one more man to split the money with. "Okay," Jack said slowly. "My men are ready. We'll finish the job today."

"Good," Mikhail replied crisply. "I have already done part of your work. The man called Havens has been eliminated."

Warren nodded, jerking his hat down. "We'll get the others," he promised, then walked away.

Mikhail watched with distaste written on his smooth-shaven face. These Americans were so coarse. Always full of bluster and threats, but squeamish when it came to backing them up.

"Hello, Mikhail. I've been looking for you."

Mikhail whirled to see a man behind him holding a pistol. Mikhail didn't know the man, but he knew Mikhail's real name. Trying to bluff his way out of it, Mikhail spread his hands in front of him and grinned apologetically. "I am sorry, Monsieur, you must have me confused with someone else. My name—"

Sergei Bronski laughed harshly. "I know who you are, and now I'm going to introduce you to the local authorities. Your gun, if you please," Bronski requested, holding out his hand.

For a wild second, Mikhail thought of trying to get the gun out in time to use it. He had no chance, so Mikhail decided to wait. A better opportunity might present itself. Moving slowly, he pulled the gun from underneath his coat and extended it to Bronski.

"Let's go see the marshal," Bronski ordered, tucking the gun under his coat.

Mikhail turned and took a small step. Holding his hands in front of him out of Bronski's sight, he slid his right hand up his left sleeve. As his fingers closed over the cold handle of the knife, Mikhail glanced over his shoulder.

"Move!" Bronski barked, taking a step forward and extending a hand to shove Mikhail.

Mikhail struck swiftly. Pulling the knife from the scabbard sewn into the lining of the sleeve, he whirled and plunged the knife into Bronski's stomach.

As Bronski's eyes widened in horror, Mikhail stabbed again and again.

Chapter Eleven

Lilly left her hotel, walking slowly down the street as she headed out to Philander's tent. Her mind deep in her own thoughts, she merely smiled absently at the greetings and compliments from the townsfolk on her singing.

The subject of her thoughts was Sergei Bronski. When she had bumped into Sergei on this very street, three days ago, she had been so glad to see him. How long since she had seen him? Twenty years? Lilly grimaced, the years reminding her that she was well into her thirties.

Still, it had been nice to see Sergei. That is, until he had requested her help. The thought of refusing never entered her mind.

Sergei was family, and one served one's family.

But now Lilly was having second thoughts. Sergei wanted her to kill for him, and to kill for the czar. Not long ago, as little as two months, Lilly would not have been bothered in the least by the thought of killing. Her only thought would have been whether or not she could profit by the killings. But now?

Lilly felt the hard outline of the Bible inside the soft purse looped around her wrist. The Bible had changed her life. For the first time in years, Lilly felt fresh and clean. The words in that book had cleansed her.

She didn't want to go back to the way she was before, but Sergei was family. Lilly stopped, oblivious to the stares she received from the people on the street.

If she ceded to Sergei's wishes and killed those men and repented, she would be forgiven. That is what the Bible said. Even one who sinned wantonly could be forgiven. If they were truly sorry for their actions and asked for forgiveness, it would be granted. Tears stinging her eyes, Lilly turned and retraced her steps back to the hotel.

A cowboy, unsteady on his feet, swept off his hat and staggered into her path. "Miss Lilly, I think you're about the purtiest thing

I ever did see. I would take it as an honor if you would marry me," he said in a slurred voice.

"Please, excuse me," she said, blindly pushing past the man. "I must go," she said, hurrying up the boardwalk.

She went into her room and tore the Bible from her purse. She glanced down at it, running her fingers lightly over the grain of the leather cover. Perhaps these men needed to die. Did that make it right? Sergei thought so. He said these men deserved to die. He said they must die. Closing her eyes, she tossed the Bible on the bed.

She turned her back on the Bible, moving stiffly to the dresser. From the top drawer, she found a pistol. Clutching the pistol to her breast, she took a deep breath. Choking back a sob, she dropped the gun into her purse. Wiping the tears from her cheeks, she opened the door. She would go find the men from Whiskey City.

Ignoring the stares we received from the folks on the busy street, Bobby and I carried Joe's body over to the stable. "What happened to him?" Cademus, the hostler, asked.

"Somebody killed him!" I said harshly.

"That's a downright shame. I am sorry,"

Cademus said hurriedly. He twisted the hammer in his hands, looking up at the high ceiling of the barn. "You can put him in the tack room for now," he offered, motioning to the back room.

We carried him into the tack room, placing him gently on a table beside the body of Nelson Buckly. I smoothed Joe's clothing, then stepped back.

"Any idea who did this?" Marshal Herndon asked from the doorway.

"Word travels fast in this town," Bobby observed.

"Yes, it does," Herndon agreed. "Especially when you carry a dead man down Main Street. Now, tell me, what happened?"

I shrugged my shoulders bitterly. "He was shot. I don't know who done it, but I got a good idea."

"Bordeaux?" the marshal asked.

"That'd be my guess," I growled.

"Mine as well," Herndon answered, running a hand across his cheek. "But all we have is suspicions. We have no hard evidence." He pointed a finger, wagging it between me and Bobby. "I don't want you two deciding to take matters into your own hands. I'll take care of Bordeaux. You stay away from him. You understand that?"

I don't reckon Bobby liked it any better than I did, but we both nodded. "Come on, Teddy," Bobby said. "I'll buy you a drink."

My mind in a kind of fog, I followed Bobby out of the stable and down to the saloon. Bobby bought a bottle and carried it over to a table. We barely got seated and our drinks poured, before Lester and Elmo rushed into the saloon. "We heard someone killed Joe!" Lester cried as they pounded over to our table.

"Yeah," I mumbled, hunched over my glass.

Elmo poured himself a drink, then glanced across the table at us. "Was it that fancy French feller?" he asked, and me and Bobby nodded. Elmo took a stiff hit from his drink, then slammed the glass down. "Well, let's go snuff the feller."

"We can't," Bobby said tiredly. He picked up the bottle and refilled his glass. "Marshal Herndon done warned us. He said he was gonna handle it."

"Aw, what's he know?" Elmo sputtered. "I say we go get that Frenchy."

I ignored Elmo, looking down in my glass. I took a quick drink, then glanced at Bobby. "Can you get the money we need from Philander?"

Bobby squirmed in his chair, swirling his glass. "Yeah, I think so," he said, but he didn't sound right sure about it. "I just haven't figured out all the details yet, but there has to be a way to use your mine as bait."

"Forget that!" Elmo blustered. "We oughta just go over there and take what we want."

"You want Marshal Herndon chasing after us all the way to San Francisco?" Bobby asked.

"He don't scare us any," Lester declared.

"Well, he bothers me," Bobby snapped. "The man's a bulldog. He'd chase us to the end of the earth. If we do it my way, we can take Philander, and it'd be months before he even knows it."

"How you gonna do that?" Lester asked, scratching his head.

"I'm not sure, yet," Bobby replied.

"Why not just sell him the mine," I suggested tiredly. "To tell the truth, I'm just about ready to get rid of the thing. It hasn't caused nothing but trouble."

"Are you crazy?" Bobby exclaimed. "That mine could be worth a fortune."

"Maybe, if I ever get a chance to work it. It'll be close to winter before we get back from California. That mine will be snowed in again," I said sourly. "We need the money now, maybe it would be best just to sell the thing to Philander."

"No, no," Bobby said hurriedly. "Don't worry, I'll think of something."

"Too bad I can't sell him my other mine," I said, refilling my glass. "All I ever got outta it was a sprung back."

"You mean that little dust hole you had outside of Whiskey City? You actually filed a claim on that?" Bobby asked, half rising from his chair.

"Yeah, a lot of good it done me," I growled. "I dug for two solid weeks and never made the price of an old shoe."

Bobby grinned. "Then, you wouldn't mind selling it?"

"Who'd buy it?" I grumbled. I picked up my glass when it finally soaked into my thick skull what he had in mind. "You're gonna tell him that's the real mine!"

"Oldest trick in the book, the old bait and switch," Bobby said, slamming the rest of his drink down. "I'll catch up with you later," he said, almost running from the saloon.

I leaned back and closed my eyes, trying to shut everything out, but the sound of Lester and Elmo arguing grated my nerves. "I'm going for a walk," I said, pushing back my chair.

"A walk?" Lester howled. "Are you all right? Why in tarnation would you want to walk on purpose?"

"I just want to think," I told them. "You guys finish the bottle."

I stepped from the saloon and saw Marshal Herndon talking to a group of folks across the street. As I approached, the group broke up. The marshal crossed his arms over his chest and waited for me to speak my piece.

"I was wondering if you could use a hand? I could help you do some asking around," I offered.

Herndon shook his head, without even considering it. "No thank you," he said curtly.

"I could help," I maintained. "After all, I am a lawman myself."

Herndon snorted and looked ready to dispute the fact, when a tall gangly man in an ill-fitting suit stepped up to us. "Marshal, might I have a word with you?"

"What is it, Blake?"

"Well, I heard you was asking if anyone saw anything strange behind the jail this morning?"

"You saw something?" I asked quickly.

"I'll ask the questions here," Herndon growled. "Now, Blake, what did you see?"

"I saw that Frenchman sneaking down the

alley from the hotel," Blake said, then spat tobacco juice into the street. "Funniest thing, he was dragging his coat behind him."

Herndon smiled, clapping the man on the back. "That's good, Blake. You'll likely have to tell this to the judge in a couple of days."

Blake shrugged. "I reckon I can do that."

"Good," Herndon grunted. "For now, I want you to keep this under your hat."

"Sure, Marshal," Blake said.

I waited until Blake was out of earshot, then asked, "You going after Bordeaux?"

"That's right," Herndon replied, pulling out his gun and spinning the cylinder.

"You want some help?"

"You?" he asked, dropping the gun back into the holster.

"Why not? I arrested fellers before."

"You mean you shot fellers, I never heard that you actually arrested anyone. I don't know how you can call yourself a peace officer. I've heard all about you, and in my book, you're just one step above a criminal yourself." Herndon stared at me coolly. "I want to arrest Bordeaux, not fill him full of holes. Now, if you will excuse me, I have an arrest to make."

Chapter Twelve

For some reason, I was drawn to the stable where Joe Haven's body lay on a table in the back room. After signing Bobby's paper, I went to be with my friend. I lost all track of time as I stood over him, my mind reliving the past.

I've seen men die, and I'm sad to say that I've even killed a few, but none of them ever affected me like this. Joe's death felt like when my parents died. I'd known Joe my whole life, and suddenly the world didn't seem right without him. I recalled how Joe gave me my first chaw of tobacco. I was sick for a week. As I stared down at the pale, waxy face, it seemed like a part of my childhood had died with him. And what of Mr. Andrews? He still hadn't woke up when I left Whiskey City. Would I return home to find out that he too had died?

"I'm sorry about your friend," Cademus said, cutting into my thoughts.

"Thanks," I said, making a couple of quick swipes at my face before turning to face the hostler. "I'm gonna miss him."

"Yeah, I bet," Cademus said.

For a second, an uneasy silence hung between us, and Cademus looked like he wished he'd never spoken. "That's a nice horse," I said, crossing to where he was grooming Bordeaux's stallion.

"It shore is," Cademus agreed, running a brush over the shiny coat.

I stroked a sleek haunch, feeling the power of muscles just under the skin. "I would like to own an animal like this someday," I said wistfully.

"Me too," Cademus said, then shook his head. "Say, you said you were looking for some horses to buy? I just bought six head this morning from a rancher up north. They're in the corral around back if you care to take a look."

I blew out a sigh, patting the stallion. I really didn't want to look at more horses, but I knew life went on. If Bobby got the money from Philander, we best be ready to move on, 'fore the reverend realized he'd been slicked.

Dragging my spurs, I shuffled out of the barn, then around to the corrals in back. The horses Cademus spoke of were good stock—part Appaloosa, judging from the dots of color splashed on their hindquarters.

As I leaned against the corral bars, a short powerful mare came to the fence, nuzzling my arm. I was rubbing between her eyes when I heard it. At first the sound registered, but it couldn't drill through my thoughts. When it came again, I finally took note.

It was a low moaning sound, like a man with a bad case of the piles. A frown on my face, I pushed away from the corral, circling around the stack of grass hay, which stood in back of the corrals. My hand on my gun, I completely circled the haystack and never saw a thing.

I was about ready to chalk it up to my imagination or the wind, when I heard it again. Scowling, I listened real hard, my eyes searching for the source of the sound. It was coming from the haystack!

"What the devil?" I muttered, dropping to one knee. As I began to dig, the sound came again, the moan of an animal in pain.

Scooping frantically, I raked hay away from the edge of the stack. In seconds, I uncovered the head of a man. I swore quickly, pulling the hay away from the man until I had him uncovered. Even as I uncovered him, I could see that I was wasting my time. It wouldn't be long until we were burying this man again.

He had a nasty bruise on his face, and a half dozen stab wounds in his chest. Ugly jagged wounds from which blood poured. I knew this man was going to die, but I was ready to fetch some help, when the man coughed and his eyes fluttered open. Strangely, when he saw me, a wistful smile fluttered across his face. "You are Teddy Cooper?" he asked, his voice heavily accented.

"Yes," I replied. Then it hit me, this man sounded like Arkady Rostov. "You're a Russian!"

"Yes," the man whispered, then smiled as my hand stole down to my gun. "Do not fear. I am not one of the men you seek. I came here to stop them."

"What do you mean?"

"I am the czar's representative to your country. I assisted Fedarov in negotiating the sale of Alaska to your country. It was one month ago, after Fedarov left, that I learned of his plans. I came immediately to the west to find him and stop him."

"How did you find out about Fedarov?"

A grimace screwed up his face as his whole body spasmed. "There are those in your country who would like to see the czar deposed. They help Fedarov. It was through them that I learned of Fedarov's true ambitions." The Russian coughed, and a froth of blood appeared on his lips. "You must stop Fedarov," he said, clutching weakly at my sleeve as I tried to use a handful of hay to slow down his bleeding. "The woman, Lilly Bronski, will help you."

"Who?" I said, too busy trying to slow down the streams of blood pouring from his chest to figure out who he meant.

The Russian almost smiled. "You know her as Lilly Simmons. Her real name is Bronski, same as my own. She will help you. She is my niece."

Lilly Simmons a Russian! I was getting more confused by the minute. Bronski spoke again, his voice so weak I could barely make it out. "You must be careful. Your life and those of your friends are in danger. There are those who would do anything to stop you."

"The Frenchman," I said slowly. "I know about him. He killed my friend."

"And me as well," Bronski said, his voice no louder than a breath of wind across a lonesome prairie. "I heard of your friend and I am sorry. The Frenchman as you call him is a vile man, but he is not French, but Russian. His real name is Mikhail Gogarian. He is the son of a prominent Russian family exiled years ago. He is a vengeful man, but he is not alone; Fedarov has hired some Americans to help him. They are led by a man named Warren."

"I'll watch out for him," I promised, working frantically, trying to press grass against the wounds, but it wasn't any use. They cut too deep into his flesh. "Don't worry about Bordeaux. The sheriff went to arrest him."

His eyes wild, Bronski grabbed my sleeve and tried to sit up. "No!" he said hoarsely. "Bordeaux is not the man you seek. It is the other one! The one called Rosseau!"

The strength ebbed from his body, and I had to catch him as he fell back. Gently I lowered his shoulders back into the soft hay as what he said sank in. Herndon was going after the wrong man!

I started to ask Bronski another question, but I noticed the peaceful look that had settled on his face. Brushing the grass from his chest, I noticed that the blood had stopped pumping from his wounds, and when I placed my ear to his chest, I could hear no heartbeat. This man was dead!

Rocking back on my heels, I turned my head, staring at the back of the hotel. Herndon was going after Bordeaux, but that was the wrong man. He wouldn't be paying any attention to Robair Rosseau. Things like that could get a man killed.

Time was running short. Bobby didn't know why this was so, but his instincts said it was. Bobby Stamper was a man who lived in tune with his instincts. They had kept him alive, and he paid heed to them.

Now, they were telling him that it was time to get out of Beaver Falls. Trouble was here. Something that they didn't understand was going on here.

His paper in his pocket, Bobby hurried over to Philander's tent. The paper was a quit claim deed that Bobby had drawn up and gotten Teddy to sign.

Bobby smiled and touched his pocket to make sure the deed was still there. He could almost picture Philander's reaction when he finally saw the hole in the dirt he was about to buy.

Bobby had no qualms about cheating a

man like Philander. In Bobby's book, a man deserved to get as good as he gave. Philander deserved to get rooked.

Flushed with the hunt, and ready for the kill, Bobby forgot about the warnings his brain was sending him. He paid little attention as he hustled out to the revival tent. He didn't notice the four sets of eyes watching him.

Jack Warren watched Bobby, then signaled to his men. Their faces hard and devoid of emotion, they loosened their guns and trailed behind Bobby.

They walked slowly, small clouds of powdered dust rising from each step. When they reached the tent, Warren pulled his gun and glanced at his men. "When I give the signal, we go in fast," he said.

A blond-haired man with a red, sunburned face, and going by the name of Sid, scowled. "What about that preacher?" he wanted to know.

Warren shrugged. "He don't matter, but if he tries to help Stamper, kill him. I want Stamper dead."

Inside the tent, Bobby and Philander stood facing each other on the small stage at the back of the tent. Bobby's face was flushed, and he was livid. "What do you mean, you're backing out?" Bobby demanded. He glanced over at Lilly, who sat at the worn piano. Was she behind Philander's sudden change of heart? Scowling, Bobby tried again. "Cooper is ready to sell. I have the quit claim right here."

"You buy him out," Philander said bluntly. "I have no time for this."

"I told you, I can't buy him out," Bobby said through tight lips. "I need your help."

"Find yourself another partner," Philander said.

"You're making a big mistake," Bobby said, fighting his temper. "This mine is worth millions."

Philander smiled. "I have received information to the contrary."

"Someone's jerking your lariat. Who told you that?"

"I did," Lilly replied quietly. Picking up her small purse from the piano, she rose gracefully to her feet. "I told the reverend that the mine was played out and not worth his trouble."

Bobby swore quickly and clenched his fists. "I knew you couldn't be trusted," he hissed.

Lilly looked ready to say something, but then all of a sudden, she pulled a gun from her purse and fired.

Chapter Thirteen

After finishing the bottle, Elmo looked hazily across the table at his brother. "You know, I don't hardly reckon Bobby's notion is gonna work," he said, his speech a little fuzzy from the whiskey.

"What do you mean?" Lester asked, running his finger around the inside of his glass, then poking it in his mouth.

"That preacher, he ain't gonna pay nothing for no played-out mine," Elmo declared.

"Sure don't sound smart to me," Lester agreed.

"Yep, a feller would have to be plumb addled to buy a mine that's all played out," Elmo said, then leaned across the table to whisper to his brother. "Now, I figure me and you are gonna have to raise that money," Elmo decided.

"Likely, you're right," Lester agreed. "You got a plan?"

Elmo grinned and nodded several times. "The way I see it, we could slip around behind that tent, cut a hole in it, then jump in and surprise that preacher. We wave our guns at him, and that do-gooder will be so scared, the money will jump outta his pockets," Elmo predicted as they left the saloon.

"Boy, yeah," Lester agreed, his speech still thick from the whiskey they had soaked up. "We'll show Bobby and Teddy. While they're pussyfootin' around, me and you will get the job done."

"Yep," Elmo said, sniffing loudly and popping his suspenders. "After we pull this off, they'll have to treat us better from now on."

They walked several yards before Lester stopped. He scrunched up his eyebrows and scratched the side of his long face. "Say, Elmo, what are we gonna do if he don't want to give up the money?"

Elmo paused, glancing back at his brother. "What do you mean?"

"I mean, what if he puts up a scrap? Cain't say as I'd feel right about drilling a preaching man."

"Preacher man my foot!" Elmo declared. "You heard what Teddy and Bobby said. He ain't no preacher man. He's just playing make-believe to trick folks outta their money."

"Oh," Lester said slowly. "So, then it would be all right to snuff him?"

Elmo dug at his nose while he thought it over. Finally, he nodded. "Sure, if he gives us any sass."

Happy with the plan, the two brothers started to circle again. They only made a few yards before the muffled sound of a shot reached them.

"What was that?" Lester whispered, grabbing his brother's arm. "Sounded like a shot to me."

"Aw, it's just some cowpoke blowing off steam," Elmo said, shrugging off Lester's worries. "Come on, let's go get that money."

Creeping along, they circled until they were directly behind the big tent. Giddy with excitement, they crept up to the tent. To anyone watching, they would have looked like kids playing. They would creep along on their stomachs, then suddenly jump up and scramble a few yards, throwing themselves back to the ground.

Out of breath, they reached the tent. Grinning at each other, they pulled their bandannas over their faces. "You got your knife?" Elmo asked, pulling his own knife and pistol.

"Right here," Lester said, pulling a foot-long bowie knife.

"Okay, on a count of three," Elmo whispered, then began to count. When he reached three, they plunged their knives into the canvas.

I figured the place to start was Bordeaux's hotel room. If Marshal Herndon went looking for the Frenchman, that'd likely be the first place he would check. If I didn't find the marshal there? Well, I would cross that bridge when I came to it.

I slid the thong off my shooter and loosened the weapon in the holster, but didn't draw it. To tell the truth, I felt a mite silly creeping down the hall, and if I was hugging onto my pistol, I'd feel even worse. I mean, for all I knew, Marshal Herndon had things well in hand.

The second I reached Bordeaux's room, I knew that wasn't so. From the hall, I could hear Robair Rosseau's voice. Now, it wasn't the same mousy voice I was used to hearing from him. No, sir, this tone was hard, with an edge of cruelty to it, but I recognized it all the same.

Now, my first instinct was to kick the door open and go in there and wring his scrawny neck, but I held back. Too many folks had been underestimating this jasper, and most of them had paid for it with their lives. I reckoned this situation called for a bit of snooping and modicum of planning.

Stooping down to one knee, I took a gander through the keyhole. First person I saw was Bordeaux. The Frenchman was backed into a corner, his hands over his head. Sprawled across the floor at Bordeaux's feet lay Marshal Herndon. The marshal's hat was gone, and I could see the jagged slash across his scalp. Blood pumped from the wound, staining the marshal's hair bright red. I didn't know if Marshal Herndon was dead or not, but he wasn't moving.

I sucked around to one side, trying to look sideways through the keyhole, but all I could see of Robair was his hand, and there was a gun in that hand. And it wasn't one of them fancy little toad shooters that Bordeaux carried, neither. No, sir, this here was a full-grown, man-size hog leg. It almost looked too big for his frail hand, but I wasn't fooled for a second. This man had killed Sergei Bronski, that man Buckly, and my friend Joe Havens.

At the memory of Joe, I almost ripped the door from its hinges and tore Rosseau's head off, but he was talking, and I dearly wanted to hear what he said.

"I am sorry, Count, but I regret to say that I shall have to terminate my employment with you," Rosseau said, sneering at Bordeaux. "I almost wish I could let you live. You do make an excellent companion. Everyone feels so sorry for me, having to put up with a vile man like you, that they never even stop to consider what I might be doing." Rosseau laughed. "You even let me plan your itinerary, so I could be here when I need to be. Yes, you've been most helpful to our cause. It's too bad I shall have to kill you."

Rosseau laughed again and took a small step forward. "Aren't you going to beg?" he taunted. "Who knows, I might spare your life."

That Bordeaux was mean and rude and 'bout as friendly as a barnyard dog, but he was also gritty as wood rasp. He didn't back up for Rosseau one bit. Even with his hands grabbing at the ceiling, he still managed to pull off that high and mighty stare. "A Bordeaux doesn't beg," he said haughtily.

Now, if you ask me, a little paddycaking and being nice woulda went a lot further, but Bordeaux didn't have it in him. Having spoke his piece, he just glared at Rosseau. I swear, if looks could kill, the one he leveled at Rosseau woulda wiped out a battalion.

For his part, Rosseau laughed harshly. "Very good," he applauded. "The royal blue blood to the end. It's a pity, really. You were so helpful, but I'm afraid I'll just have to kill you both."

I wasn't gonna let that happen. I backed away a couple of steps and was all set to charge that door when a shot rang out.

I musta jumped ten feet in the air. I went to grabbing my belly and patting myself down when I realized that I hadn't been shot. Scrambling back to the door, I mashed my eye up to the keyhole. Neither Bordeaux nor Herndon had been shot.

I was still puzzling what happened, when I heard Rosseau chuckle. "I would say that was the end of Bobby Stamper. Some of my associates saw him going into Reverend Philander's tent and decided to pay their respects."

A lone, mournful shot rang out, its echo hanging in the air like smoke over a prairie fire. Rosseau laughed. "Bobby Stamper was in the right place. I would say a preacher is exactly what he needs right now."

As if to back Rosseau's words, a raft of shots ripped through the town.

Chapter Fourteen

Bobby had never trusted Lilly, but the last thing he expected was for her to come out with a gun and go to blasting. As fire blasted from the end of the gun, his life didn't flash in front of him, but he did have a fleeting thought about his wife, Betsy, as he braced for the impact that never came.

She missed! Even as that thought raced through his mind, Bobby heard a cry from behind him. He started to turn and saw the blur of a rifle butt streaking at his head. he managed to duck a little, but the rifle still smashed into his shoulder, knocking him to the dirt floor of the tent.

As Bobby rolled to the floor, Jack Warren leaped onto the small stage and ripped the gun from Lilly's hand. For a second the tent was deathly still as everyone caught their breath. Sid shuffled over to Bobby, taking his gun and giving him a boot in the ribs.

"Hank, are you all right?" Warren asked, glancing at the man Lilly shot.

"I'll live," Hank muttered, trying to wrap his bandanna around his bleeding arm. He swore, glaring at Lilly as he flipped blood from his fingers.

"I'll let you kill her for that," Warren said with a harsh laugh. "If you folks know any prayers, you best be saying them now," he said, raising his gun.

Warren's men were ready to shoot, when the man standing next to the canvas wall at the rear of the tent screamed. He took a staggering step forward, then fell to his knees, a large knife protruding from his back.

Warren swore viciously and whirled to face the back of the tent. As if by magic, Elmo's face and arm appeared through a hole in the tent. "Grab some sky!" he squawked, the bandanna slipping from his face. "This is a hold—" Elmo's words ended in a bleat as he realized that the hole wasn't big enough and he was stuck.

As the guns swung toward him, Elmo screamed and tried to worm back out of the hole; he could not. The reason he couldn't was Lester. Having lost his knife, Lester figured the best way he could help was to shove Elmo on through the hole. He was behind his brother, his boots spinning in the dust as he pushed on Elmo's backside with all his might.

As Warren and his men spun to face the new threat, Bobby reacted. Diving across the stage, he tore the gun loose from the stabbed man. Rolling on his shoulder, Bobby came smoothly into a kneeling position. Leveling the gun at Warren, Bobby fired. Thumbing back the hammer, Bobby slammed another bullet into Warren as the gunman fell.

Sid and Hank were in trouble. Two of their number were already dead, and now they faced an enemy from both sides. When it counted, they hesitated. That small hesitation proved their undoing.

As they stood frozen, Bobby swung his pistol at Sid and fired three times. The bullets smashed Sid back, driving him into the pulpit. Even as Sid tripped over the pulpit, Bobby was swiveling on his knee, bringing the gun to bear.

Slowed by the bullet in his left arm, Hank was still trying to line up a shot, when Bobby pulled the trigger. Click. The gun was empty!

Hank smiled and was taking dead aim at Bobby when the bullet struck him. Elmo hadn't meant to fire; his only concern was beating a hasty retreat. He flailed his arms, trying to grab something for leverage, when he accidentally pulled the trigger. The bullet struck Hank in the back, knocking him to the floor.

After the shots died away, even Elmo's screams sounded quiet. As the smoke from the shots drifted slowly up to the ceiling, Bobby lunged to his feet.

He was moving to help Elmo, when the canvas split all the way to the floor, spilling Elmo into the tent like water from an overturned barrel.

Elmo slammed into the ground, his gun going off as his hand was jarred by the fall.

"Dang it, Elmo, hold still!" Bobby screamed, then ripped the pistol from his hand.

"Is it safe to come in?" Lester called anxiously from outside.

"Yeah, come in," Bobby said with a grunt, grabbing Elmo by the back of the shirt and jerking him to his feet. "Here, be careful with this thing," he admonished, stuffing the gun down into Elmo's holster.

"I don't know what you're so surly about,"

Elmo squawked. "Reckon me and Lester saved your sorry hide."

Bobby wanted to deny the fact, and even started to do it; then he stopped, chuckling softly. "Yeah, I guess you did at that," he acknowledged, and turned to Lilly. "What's your story, lady? Were you shooting at them or me?"

"Why, them, of course," Lilly said. "I was only trying to help you."

"Then why did you tell him that Teddy's mine was no good?" Bobby demanded. "We needed that money."

Lilly glanced at Philander, who still looked pale and shaken. "He was going to cheat you. That mine is worth more than four hundred dollars. I had some of the ore from it tested; it is very rich in silver."

"We knew that," Bobby said disgustedly. "We weren't gonna sell him that mine. We were gonna sell him another worthless hole in the ground."

"What!" Philander screamed. He jumped forward, raising his finger, but a scowl from Bobby silenced him.

"Shut up," Bobby said. He glanced down at the dead men, then up at Lilly. "Why did you take a potshot at them?"

"I knew they were here to kill you. They

were hired to keep you from making it to California."

"Why didn't you tell us that before?" Bobby roared.

"Would you have believed me?" Lilly shot right back.

Bobby grinned wryly and rubbed his chin. "Not likely," he admitted. "But you coulda tried."

Lilly cast her eyes down at the floor. "I wanted to, but I was told not to."

"Who told you that?"

"My uncle. He is Russian. He serves the czar. He told me all about the plot against the czar and how you and Teddy were involved. He said these men were sent here to stop you. I wanted to warn you and Teddy, but he said no. He said they had an accomplice. He didn't want you killing these men before he learned who the accomplice was."

"Bordeaux!" Bobby exclaimed.

"No it was the other one. The one called Rosseau."

Bobby didn't move for a second, then he swore bitterly and took off at a dead run.

Chapter Fifteen

I was so stunned, I just seemed to freeze in place. I stared down the long, empty hallway. Bobby was in trouble, and he needed my help.

I almost unhinged my head, I whipped it around so many times trying to figure out what to do. If I left to go help Bobby, Rosseau would almost certainly kill Herndon and Bordeaux before I could get back, and I didn't even know if Bobby needed me. For all I knew, he had won the fight, or he might already be dead.

I guess I knew all along what I had to do, I just never liked it any. My duty was to the marshal and Bordeaux. I had to trust Bobby to take care of himself. I knew Bobby was a mighty sly man. The kind of goons Rosseau had working with him would be in for the ride of their lives when they locked horns with Bobby Stamper.

Feeling a slight better, I heard Rosseau blabbing off at the mouth again. "In a few seconds, you will be joining Stamper, then I shall hunt down that oaf Cooper and make a clean slate of it."

Wanted a piece of me, did he? Well, I'd be tickled to oblige. I backed off to the far side of the hall. Now, I know it might not look thataway, but I weren't just jumping in blind. Nope, I had myself a plan.

I reckon it shoulda worked too.

The thing that fouled me up was that danged door. I figured to wallop into it and knock it open with my shoulder. From there, I planned to barrel on in and snare Rosseau round the neck and squeeze till his head popped off.

The thing was, that door was flimsy as wrapping paper. Why, a good spit wad woulda knocked a hole in it, and I'm a big man. And I hit that door at a high gallop.

Instead of busting open and swinging outta my way, the blasted thing just disintegrated into a shower of splinters. I swear, I ran right through the thing!

Splinters gouged my eyes and tore at my face, plumb near blinding me. I couldn't see Rosseau, so instead of snatching onto him, I brushed right past him and smacked face first into the wall.

Now, that door hadn't slowed me down a whit, and I still had a fair charge of motivation behind when I kissed that wall. I swear, I slapped into that wall so hard, I durn near tipped the whole building over. After planting my faceprint in the wall, I bounced back like a silver dollar off a feather bed.

That's where ol' Robair made his mistake. If he woulda throwed down with that pistol and commenced to blazing away, he'd likely killed me good and proper. Instead, he took a swipe at my noggin with that shooter. Now, it hurt like the devil, but I got a right thick skull and he didn't catch me solid. The short of it was, he didn't put me down, he just wobbled my knees a mite.

My eyes all glazed over and watering like a set of rapids, I latched onto his gun hand. I wanted to curl my other arm round his neck, but he hauled off and butted me square in the face.

Now that hurt! Right about then, it sorta dawned on me that I was in a dog-eat-dog fight, and if I gave this man half a chance, he was gonna kill me.

'Fore I could get a head of steam built, Rosseau tromped down on my toes with the heel of his boot, then drove a fist into my belly. Gasping for air, I doggedly held onto his gun hand and tried to circle my arm around his neck for a headlock.

He never gave me a chance to get set. He butted me again, then whacked me open-handed across the ear. Bells rang in my ears as I clung to him, trying to keep my feet.

Through the ringing in my ears, I heard him laugh. "I'll kill you, just like I killed your friend."

A flashing picture of Joe shot through my mind, and a rage surged through my body. All of a sudden, I wasn't fighting just to stop this man, I wanted to kill him! To maim him, then kill him.

Letting out a beller, I left off trying for a headlock and drove the point of my elbow right into his kisser. That snapped him back and gave me a chance to lift my knee up into a right good spot. When my knee crashed into his groin, he let out a croaking sound and sorta went limp. Now, I reckon, if I woulda swatted him a good one in the chops, that woulda been the end of it.

The thing was, I was mad. My face and eyes were burning like a bonfire. I was mad and in pain. Plus, this man killed a friend of mine. I reckon I was half outta my mind.

I grabbed him by the scruff of the neck and the seat of the britches, hauling him plumb off the ground. Bellering like a bull moose, I charged at the window. Heaving with all my might, I pitched him headlong out the window.

He crashed through the glass, screaming like a scalded dog. A dull thud cut off his screams.

Feeling like burnt porridge, I staggered over to the window. My chest heaving like a fireplace bellows, I looked down at Rosseau. He'd lit smack-dab on his gourd, and from the way his head was twisted back underneath him, I could tell his neck was broken.

I can't say that I was gonna shed any tears for the varmint, but I was sorry it had to be me that killed him. 'Course, he had it coming.

All of the anger and energy draining right out of me, I staggered backwards, then sat down heavily. I could see Marshal Herndon stirring, so I knew he wasn't dead, but he wasn't exactly up to turning cartwheels neither. I figured I oughta help him up, but I couldn't find the gumption to do it. I was still sitting there on the floor, my head sagging down to my chest, when Bobby rushed in.

"Is everybody all right?" he shouted.

"I guess so," I said and grunted, not ready to commit to anything just yet. I raised my head as Lester and Elmo crowded in behind Bobby. "Rosseau said his men were gonna ambush you!"

Bobby laughed, giving Herndon a hand to his feet. "They tried their dangdest, but they never had a chance. Not when I had Lester and Elmo on my side."

Elmo hooked his thumbs in his gun belt and took a strutting step forward. "Yeah, we cooked their hash real good," he bragged, then paused, shooting a guilty look at Bobby. " 'Course, Stamper helped some too," he mumbled.

Marshal Herndon staggered over to the window. Holding a hand to his bloody head, he looked down at Rosseau for a long time. I braced myself for the tongue-lashing I knew was coming. Marshal Herndon surprised me though. He didn't look at all mad as he turned away from the window. He even managed a little chuckle. "I'll say one thing for you boys, you don't do things by halves." He shook his head and extended a hand down to me. "I guess I have to take back what I said, you're a real peace officer," he said, hauling me up to my feet. For a second our eyes met, then Herndon smiled. "And I want the lot of you outta my town."

"We'd like to go, marshal, but . . ." I stopped glancing at Bobby. "Did Philander?"

"No, he backed out of the deal," Bobby said with a sad shake of his head.

"I'm sorry, Marshal," I said. "But we're short of horses and dead broke. I don't reckon we can leave."

Herndon frowned, and I thought he was gonna tear his mustache loose from his face, he was pulling at it so hard. "Maybe we could pass the hat," he said slowly. "I'm betting folks in this town would pitch in. I'd gladly kick some in, if it would get you on your way."

"That won't be necessary," Bordeaux said quietly. He pushed away from the wall and crossed the room, walking with stiff dignity. "I feel as if part of this is my fault," he said, then turned and held out his hand. "You saved my life, Monsieur. This I do not forget. From this day forward, your debts are my own. Purchase whatever you need. I shall see that it is paid for."

I took that to mean he was gonna pay for

our truck, and I pumped his hands. "That's right kind of you," I said.

The next morning, as the sun was just beginning to hint of a new day, we led our horses out of the stable. My own hand was wrapped around the reins of Bordeaux's big bay stallion.

In the end, Bordeaux had heard how much I admired the horse and insisted that I take the animal—not that I resisted too much.

That Bordeaux, he was a funny feller. Stiffer than an oak board, he was generous when he took the notion. Fact is, I was getting to where I kinda liked him.

There was dew on the grass and peace in the air as we walked slowly up the hill toward the cemetery. In the vague light, I could see Marshal Herndon and Lilly waiting beside the open graves, their heads bowed as they waited.

The four of us left our horses outside the gate, then joined Lilly and the marshal by the graves. As we lowered Joe and Bronski into their last bed, Lilly spoke a simple sermon. She wasn't no real preacher, but her words were sweet and sincere, and I reckon Joe woulda liked them. After she finished, we began covering the graves. Her voice soft as the wing of a dove, Lilly sang a hymn while we worked.

As her voice trailed off, I patted the fresh mound of dirt. "Rest easy, my friend. I'll be thinking of you from time to time."

As I straightened up, we all shifted our feet, not wanting to leave just yet. It seemed like we should do more, but we'd done all that could be done.

Finally, we shook hands with Herndon and swung aboard our horses. We turned our backs to the rising sun and rode slowly away from Beaver Falls. California awaited us.